This signed, li

THE SURF

is one of only 200 copies and is

number 150

SATELLITES

THE SURF

First published 2022 by Solaris
an imprint of Rebellion Publishing Ltd,
Riverside House, Osney Mead,
Oxford, OX2 0ES, UK

www.solarisbooks.com

ISBN: 978 1 78618 806 9

Copyright © Kwaku Osei-Afrifa 2022

The right of the author to be identified as the author
of this work has been asserted in accordance with the Copyright,
Designs and Patents Act 1988.

All rights reserved. No part of this publication may be
reproduced, stored in a retrieval system, or transmitted,
in any form or by any means, electronic, mechanical,
photocopying, recording or otherwise, without the prior
permission of the copyright owners.

This is a work of fiction. All the characters and events
portrayed in this book are fictional, and any resemblance
to real people or incidents is purely coincidental.

10 9 8 7 6 5 4 3 2 1

A CIP catalogue record for this book is available
from the British Library.

Designed & typeset by Rebellion Publishing

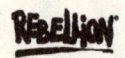

Printed in the UK

THE SURF

Kwaku Osei-Afrifa

SOLARIS

*For Jorge.
Come we go.*

THE RULES OF ULTSURF

- Ultsurf is a race to get through six hexagonal gates, known as Splits, in the correct order that the gamemaster designates in the fastest time possible.
- Each team plays with a squad of 64 players: Escorts, Greys, Slip, Speed—broken into 32, 12, 12, 8.
- All players must pass through the splits during the game.
- 32 players must be in play at all times; breaking that down into a formation amongst the four squads is down to the team's discretion.
- Escorts make up half a team's roster and are there to defend everyone else.
- Greys are a disruptive squad, intending to slow down the opposing players' progress and time throughout the game area.
- The Slip squad act to propel the Speeds across the game area.
- The Speed squad are the fastest of any team and act as the primary scorers.
- A Speed's time through a split is the most valuable to a team's chance at victory.
- When a split is active, the time for every squad in play is running.
- The team that gets all their Speeds through a live split first 'own' it and that counts as a point towards victory.
- Alternatively, the team with the fastest recorded time for a Speed's passage can steal it from the opposing team's score.

The Surf

- Once the entire Speed squad have all logged times, the team cannot score with that split again.
- The team that own the most splits by the end of the game win.
- If the score is tied by the end of the game, the order of finish moves to the combined times through all splits (if there are more than two teams competing in the same game).
- Therefore, it is possible to have a slower combined time during the game but still emerge victorious if a team has owned splits through the fastest Speed through scoring mechanism.
- In the rare event that a game's duration extends beyond one hour, the game is paused and must be decided in overtime at a designated secondary game area. Teams will have only one split to contend over.
- A team may participate in as many games as it can in the allocated match window, however, the more games a team competes in, the greater risk they run for their times and scores on the season.
- There is no limit to how many teams can compete in one game area, but there must be two teams at the start for the game to commence.
- Contact is unavoidable and allowed during play.
- Teams must provide the gamemaster with an appropriate medical plan in case of player injury or fatality.
- It is incumbent on every team to have their exit strategy in place in the event of a game stoppage by the authorities. A safe zone rendezvous will be made available dependent on the game area's location and

its coordinates are shared with team leaders and team leaders only, to keep the flow of information contained.
- Any team leader found disclosing locations before the stoppage of a game will have their team forfeit the game, be suspended from participating in the next game, and risk the potential of more severe sanctions—like disqualification for them solely, or collectively as a team—if the act is found to be an egregious fault.

Falling.

That's the bit you learn last to let go. It's funny because you'd think they'd tell you about it first. Day one. Sitting in pre-flight and Gunny hands everyone a bucket as they file in, sit down. Gunny, at this point, also tells everyone not to ask any questions. Not now. Not ever. Not till we lose our tails. He calls us tadpoles.

Another thing, we're in flight suits with a detachable tail, so we do kinda look like tadpoles.

The name stuck and we adopted it as our team identity. Our shuttle is one of twins docked inside a large plane, a bulbous hunk of windowless metal. It's a smooth take-off, the board is green, speed is accelerating towards nominal. All the efficiency of routine. So why am I gritting my teeth and squeezing my eyes closed? My hands inside their gloves feel clammy and overly big. I feel toes spring out from the webs between my already-toes, and I'm waiting for my boots to burst all bone, sinew, extra toes and the smell. When we level out at our desired altitude, that sensation of not-moving sets in, my teeth relax, and I pull faces to restore feeling in my jaw.

I look down at my feet and there's no carnage. I thank the Sun.

There's a slapping, wet sound and I think that's the first person to lose their breakfast. A green face lifts from out of the bucket, there's a sheen of sweat and some debris in the tousled blonde hair on top of his head and around his mouth. I've never liked beards, no that's not quite right, I *hate* beards.

We're being pressed into our seats under three gees. We're strapped in harnesses with just enough freedom of movement to lift bucket, lower head, return head to rest, and hyperventilate based on the breathing patterns around me. And from me, I'm ashamed to say.

A LIGHT TURNS from red to blue above us. We eight-by-eight strong look up as an earpiece is ejected from a panel beside our left ears. I lean into mine and sixty-three others do the same. Once the niggly little bud is in my ear, I stop leaning. Last week I was here and I didn't stop leaning and I had the *worst* crick in my neck. They didn't let me out of the shuttle. The twin shuttle let out another version of me, a fellow Speed with middling times, and I had to stay here and watch everyone Surf.

Watching the Surf doesn't suck per se, but watching people Surf when you should be out there sucks. It *really* sucks.

Especially when you have to sit through watching a loss.

I'm determined to be crick-free today and thankfully—or mercilessly depending on who you ask—it's actually a warmer and, believe it or not, a brighter day. Maybe it was destiny to miss last week. Some of the tadpoles around me have clocked my trick with the earbud, and have tried to sit back in rest position with it in place. A couple of them have managed it. I incline my head in approval. One girl, acne-ridden and with one hell of an overbite, has dropped her bud, eyes wide in worry. I reckon she wants to tell Gunny, but what's he really gonna do other than get really mad at her for fucking up this early? She's at the end of my row, and if this briefing isn't as long as the last one, then maybe I'll have time to give her broad strokes before we Surf.

"Tadpoles," Gunny's voice is clear; I can't hear any of the gees on him, and I'm pretty sure I spend all my energy trying to keep my face off of the floor, "pre-flight prep is almost complete. We're two klicks from the cluster of impact zones we're looking to Surf. There are five other teams kicking around looking for a break, and our sky bitch has warned me that if we don't time it right, the traffic will be heavy, and it'll get dangerous and people might die."

Cue a couple gasps and another wet slap in a bucket.

I think about Polly, the cloudchaser (or 'sky bitch' dependent on who you ask) back at base camp, grounded, and I wonder who the joke's on.

"Your flight suit has been modified after the last Surf the team did. We've stuck as close to regulation as we can, but if we don't bend the rules, we don't get wins. We don't get points, we don't move up the table, you don't get paid and my husband gives me a hard, fucking time." We hazard the chest-constricting act of laughing. It goes well. We receive no retaliation from gravity or Gunny. He continues. "Keep to the formations in your playbook and no one should wipe out. There are some new starters, sound off please."

"Bellamy, check."

"Ava, check."

My turn. "Elerie, check," and I'm proud I get every syllable out evenly.

"Darius, check."

"James the Better, check."

"James the Lesser, check."

"Field of play in thirty," the pilot says over the comms, "bottoming out," and there is a whoosh and the sound of the outside comes in fast. Our feet dangle as the floor falls away. Breathers activate once the cabin depressurises. We're sat in columns of eight, and it's a time-delayed release from the outside in. We're at the zenith of the planet's atmosphere. I'm in the middle two columns and we're the Speed team. It's our split times that'll get us either the most or least points. It's also the crew with the highest mortality rate. I think that was meant to dissuade me from my latest obsession, but I'm five minutes from hurtling out of a shuttle tens of thousands of feet above the ground for the third time just this month, so I don't think it went all that well to be honest.

I've got my leash between my legs, and before that thought can go any further, the first team are loosed.

They're Escorts for the whole crew. Fifteen seconds later, another team are deployed and there's a clanking before someone cries out that they're covered in shit. Bearded bucket man didn't deposit his sick like he was supposed to. That'll be it. Amateur. I hope he dies out there. I know three of the Slip team who are due next. They're meant to seek out impact clusters, slingshotting the Speed crews between them. The Jameses are Slippers and their double act extends out in the air. The third Slipper, everyone called her Nobility on the account of her accent, unbelievable wardrobe, and the fleet of beautiful humans who accompanied her everywhere except up here in the Surf. I'm sure, given the option, those humans would be up here instead of us: following their queen wherever she went. I can't tell if I want the entourage or to be in it.

"Speed, we're running Dagger formation."

Wait, what? That takes my thoughts right from social status to right where it needed to be.

"Dagger wasn't in the playbook today."

"I know, but we've practiced it before and it's fast."

"It's also fucking dangerous if we're not *all* in sync."

Slip are out, and we have a minute to sort out this domestic.

"Dagger's the best for Slip; the other teams won't catch us if we do it right."

If we do it right.

"Yeah, if we do it right, and I'm not betting my skull on whether you testie heavies can get it right," that's Ava talking. She hates men, like full on hates men. She's one of those descended from descendants of Amazon tribes. I like her, but tradition can take a backseat at Mach One, y'know?

"And it's what Lesser thinks!"

"Fuck Lesser, he was *Phalanx*. You can't trust him."

"Seriously?"

"Yeah!"

"Even after we played them?"

"That proved nothing…"

"What's the new girl say? She'd be the tip of the dagger after all!"

"Uh—" Now no one else was yelling. It was just me. The new girl.

"Take your time, rook, it's not like we're dropping any second now."

Ugh, sarcasm, I don't need this right now. I'm trying to remember my routes.

Five.

Four.

Three.

Two.

"I'm feeling sharp!" and the metal interior of the shuttle was now the hot, gusty air of the Surf. Oh shit, that poor, scared girl from before. Probably hurtling through the air at mach speed, out of formation and without a single clue of what to do. I wouldn't be surprised if she was scraped off the ground at close of play.

THERE'S A CONTRACT all players are meant to sign at the start of the season. It's basically life insurance. Ultsurf is a hazardous sport and operates in this thin, grey area between a bloodsport and a sport that often ends with blood being spilled—in the system, there are only three planets who haven't outlawed, or in some cases sanctioned, Ultsurf. A squad is made up of four crews: Greys, Escorts, Slip and Speed. Escorts make up half of any team's players. It's in the name what they are there to do, and it's no accident that there are enough Escorts for every other crewmember, but I don't think I've ever seen a team deploy a formation like that. Then the Greys hurtle through the air wearing sterner armour and wielding batons to interrupt—or kill, more accurately—the flight plan of Speeds like me. The anti-Escort, if you will. Mix that with adrenaline and the need to win, players get injured and regularly die. The life insurance and accompanying non-culpability clause says even though loved ones may be financially remunerated upon your untimely death, it would be in instalments so continued silence was encouraged. And it wasn't an amount that meant you could pack in all responsibility, buy yourself a moon somewhere, and play zero-grav golf till the end of your days.

Eventually, I was hosing myself down in my shower, my body its own solar system of bruises, gashes, and welts. Us Tadpoles had lost again. And the water pressure was absolutely getting worse. By the Sun, it was a pitiful season, but my numbers were up again after this game. If I could keep this up for the remaining games, then maybe come the off-season, I could find myself on another team. A better team. The Jameses kept me in play, finding impact clusters like it was second nature to them. A bond not all that old, but all that synchronised. I didn't know how they did it. It took me *ages* to like anybody, let alone someone I had to trust with my life… Gunny made me a Speed because ballet. But he definitely didn't check the file all that deeply because the only ballet I did was my pre-preparatory exam. That I failed. When I was five. And I was a fat, ungainly blob who hated every moment in that leotard. So I didn't devote my still-forming anatomy to that brutish sport, and instead committed my barely-formed body to this devilish game. Now my split times and scores were in the upper bracket of the league. And, maybe, ballet might've been a better choice…

Our game was undetected, and mostly complete, until some clever shit got knocked seriously off-course, and he flagged surface-to-air radar detection of an airport. Which was mostly a miracle considering there were five other teams in play by then. We had to hotfoot it the hell out of there. Most of the teams made for the ground. The rendezvous a decommissioned military base that was now a public museum. Just slip into the tours, stow your gear and pretend like you give a shit about the Terran Civil War, that iterations of the Martian Raptor interceptor fighter were simply to *die for*. Who cares if we were all old enough to sire the usual clientele at this time of the day.

I took a hard pass for the military base and risked detection to stay in the air just that bit longer: I had the Jameses slingshot me one last time and I Surfed from impact zone to impact zone for kilometres before I got picked up. I loved when I was up there, away from the shit down there, away from any responsibility. Anyone rich enough to fuck with the lottery of transhuman capabilities that doesn't choose flight is a sundamned idiot and has never Surfed. Choose invisibility if you never want to wear clothes ever again, sure, if that's what you're into. Choose immortality if you like being lonely for, like, fucking forever. But if you wanted to touch the divine, really understand some of the galaxy we called our home, fly. And that's what I did. No hunting impact zones, no game, no Gunny, no split times, no risk of a Grey trying to eat me alive. Just the HUD telling me where I was, how hot I was getting, and how the race between arrest and extraction was going. We were all sanctity of life, deified design in most situations. Things. Just. Were. Feeling or identifying be damned. But once you commodified the human genome, made it malleable like a kid's toy, subject to enhancement like a patch in a program's code we flocked, we flocked. Maybe that's what it took: for nothing to be off-limits so that everything could be okay. That people like me could be less the weirdos tampering with what's 'meant to be'.

I was verging on severe heatstroke and had burns inside my suit when I literally peeled it off. My tadpole tail made it through the journey mostly intact. I'd taken a hard landing near a public pool and I bounced into it to the shock, and some glee, of the assembled sunbathers and swimmers. The steam my suit made when I broke the surface was a *picture*. Ugh, any repairs were gonna come directly out of my salary, and that was shit because my studio's AC was on the fritz and the days weren't getting any colder. Outside of Ultsurf and thinking about Ultsurf I didn't get out much. Most of the friends I grew up with were off-world, like *actually* off-world, making slingshots all over the system with their high-paid jobs, wives, husbands, and romantic communes. But one relic from my life had surfaced and I was meeting her later, hence the hosing down: I was scrubbing up nicely for India Palmer, former collegiate President, class of 2244's most likely to succeed—and succeed she had. The matriarch of a biotech conglomerate corporation mainly responsible for extending our life expectancy into the hundreds.

I put myself in a baggy jumpsuit and packed plenty of water. I fiddled with wearing my spex and blinked all the way from my studio to the monorail. The windows' filters were right up to match my spex's settings, and I was grateful for the break from the sun sun sun. As I sat watching the world murkily zip by, I remembered my mother's explanation of moving to this world. They promised us riches, so she participated in our old quadrant's ballot for the three of us to go. Winners got an expense-paid relocation settlement to Aurin. It wasn't instant, or quick, or an easy process. Not for us or anyone around us neither. I didn't know the word at the time, but there was a *fugue* that settled onto our immediate world. Like those graphics of odours settling on your fabrics in advertising vids. Or a rootkit running in sync, in shadow, underneath a system if you're tech-savvy and find the mating call of capitalism odious.

People got meaner to each other. Now I'm not sure if opinions on our neighbours affected outcomes, but did that stop you keeping tabs on your proximals? How societally useful they were, did they recycle? Did they volunteer? Never run a red light on their bikes? Of course it didn't. The not-knowingness, that ineffable question gnawed chunks off friendships, marriages, congregations and comprehensively reconfigured any collection of humans above a group size of one. I had a best friend who journaled endlessly about this time in our lives. He shared them with me and Tosin as alpha readers before he started posting them online. Despite our expert feedback and his devotion, they never gained that much traction—I always thought because they were shit but Jonah, bless him, maintained his pieces were 'confiscated by the powers that be' as he was 'too close to the truth', and when I told him 'no one likes an oracle, look what happened to Cassandra,' he didn't talk to me for approximately nineteen days, and I learnt a valuable lesson about never throwing shade on his art and his feelings—and I never shook his memorable phrase of the 'Aurin Audit' from any part of me.

I was a littler thing then and it stretched my capacity to picture *another* world. Like this one, but different. Newer. Nicer. And not for just everyone. But eventually, mother and I moved here fifteen years ago. I stopped talking to her eight years ago.

I stepped off the monorail, weaving my way through evening commuters either going home or scrubbed up nicely for their own evening engagements. A lot of them, the real high-rollers, weren't wearing spex at all. Idly gliding by, looking like nothing doing, like Aurin's constant daylight was as unremarkable as breathing. When you got close enough, or they turned their heads to catch the light, you could see the glint of their lenses. The lenses changed with your eyes. Real rich, fancy shit.

Yeah but were any of you in the sunkissed sky earlier? I think not!

I wouldn't have to wear the spex for long, though. Mine weren't the latest model. India gave me the address of this swish eatery when I was at home and I spat out my noodles when the location flashed up on my slate. No great loss; the noodles weren't the best. She was taking me to North Ombro. The Ombros are practically where high-rollers are *made* and spend all of their time. Seeing a *night sky*. I was fanning myself at the prospect of spending an evening free from sweat, heat, stickiness, humidity. She'd cleared an Ombro visitor code, and it synced with me on the monorail over. I caught myself rubbing my neck in anxiety as I walked towards the Ombro checkpoint.

What if this was some joke a teammate was playing on me? What had it been: years, close to a decade, since I'd spoken to India? Hold on, why only now, moments from the checkpoint did it finally occur to me that this could be a ruse? That I was a rat in a fucking maze and what looked like the way out was actually the cat's open mouth, thrilled that dinner was volunteering itself?

Those assembled by the checkpoint looked me up and down. It took a lot not to react. If anything, their looks confirmed what I was too stupid to realise before now. I couldn't turn around though, pretend I was lost or some shit. I had joined the back of a queue and more people joined me, so I was no longer the back. No easy means of escape now... You only come here when you're *invited* here, when you *belong* here. And I'd had some delusion that maybe an invitation was mine today. But as my ankle almost gave way under me once more, that was a clearer indication of why they were staring. My limp. My body still bruised; constellations of welts and lacerations mostly covered by the jumpsuit. My sister's make-up tutorials didn't quite cover how to contour breather mask cheek lines or, worse, the spex-rings. The last few steps—if I could stretch my amble to be called 'steps'—took me to a checkpoint guard and her scanner. A crisp, finely pressed evening-sky-blue uniform with a sun decal on the shoulders. I have such 'an artistic disposition' that I focused on what the guard was wearing, and not the machine gun lazing in her arms. Maybe this was a bad idea? Not that options were rushing to present themselves to me at my time of need. I didn't know what to do either. So I tried to watch what the people around me were doing. Their actions I could copy, but that ease, that confidence they moved with was beyond me. The guard beckoned me forward, gesture clipped with annoyance, all jerk and no grace or welcoming to succour like every commercial vid said. For holding up the line behind me. I glanced over my shoulder and it was long. There was another checkpoint person, stood in front of one of those screens where, on my side, I can look right through, but on their side they could see everything. Similar sun decal on the shoulders, but he was in a uniform the pinkish-orange of a sunset. Eventually I leaned forward, swiping my Minul over the sensor. And India's visitor code flashed on my Minul. Thank the sunblessed Sun! Neither guard checked their surprise quick enough. The screen guard apologised, overcompensated by telling me to keep warm too nicely, and sent me on my way. Jerky-Arm left her disbelief plain for me to see, though. Asshole.

The spex went into my coat pocket as I drew the whole thing around me; knew I brought it for a reason. I rubbed at my abused eye sockets; tried to massage into them the clean, clear, smooth skin of someone who hadn't spent almost half of her life squinting. Did I want a bigger sign hovering overhead declaring that I didn't belong? Ugh. I willed my hands still. Took a swig of water. Warm. I think I need a new bottle. Sundamned thing almost never kept anything cold. Another excuse to fidget. I need to stop. Back to my hands. I held my wrist with the other hand behind my back and attempted something approaching calm. Decided that the only angst I could get away with was internal. Introspect only; to project was to evoke sunlight on your problems. So garish, so *boring*. The change in Ombro was almost immediate. It *looked* like night now. Felt like it too. Part of me wanted to gaze skyward and see the 'stars'. But it would probably have my brain leaking out of my nose in seconds.

Considering the old-timer pose I was rocking, it was probably too late. Brain matter had long since departed for freedom from their cranial detention. Instead, I buttoned up my jacket, thrust my hands into the pockets and made for Nox.

INDIA WAS PLUMPER than I remembered. Then again, she was older than I remembered too. Why she had got back in touch with me when she did, I had no idea. Highrollers played by their own rules. She had this laugh that seemed like it was coming out of this tiny place where the old India I grew up knowing was still alive. I realised I liked watching her laugh. And making her laugh. I was on my third large glass of wine and was ready to tell her about my secret crush on her little brother. Lightweight in all walks of my life. India was knocking them back, but she didn't look how I felt. From our booth suspended above the main restaurant floor, I could see everyone else glitter in their finery. We had satellite booths and the high-backed chairs and walls made us all tiny private islands.

I pushed my plate forward and wiped my hands and mouth to stop licking my fingers. A satisfied sigh escaped my lips, leaning back cradling my new food baby. India was smiling this smile I couldn't work out over the top of her wine glass, but fuck it I didn't care. I'd shoved so much high-roller grub down my throat, and she kept swiping *her* Minul to pick up the bill.

"Somebody enjoyed her food?" Any trace of her old lisp had been eradicated. Power, I guessed.

"You high-rollers know how to indulge," I said between gouging morsels from between my teeth with a toothpick.

India rolled her eyes, but that laugh came back and I felt it in my stomach. "You're still calling them high-rollers eh, Ele?"

I did a scoff that was altogether disgusting. "*Them*? More like you. Look where we are. Look at that fucking asteroid belt around your neck!" Plus she was wearing, *wearing*, her Minul as part of her jewellery. Sane people like me have it locked away with secure, *remote* access. I call them totems—unique items chosen for sentimental or inconspicuous value mapped to your biometrics to ensure another layer of security. They had an official (which I knew was more boring) name, but I liked totems much better. Sadly, it wasn't catching on. I would always have to explain, and then the person would say 'ooooh, why didn't you just say that in the first place?' and I would want to punch them in the throat and say 'ooooh, why don't you just choke and die?' But never would I *actually throw* the punch. Once or twice I came close. Anyway, your Minul contains absolutely everything about you and how cavalier she was with it was probably high-roller 101 but so completely badass I couldn't drag her for it.

"Are you going to hold that against me? We wouldn't be here..." She did this expansive gesture, taking in our luxurious surroundings. She looked well at home doing that, and there wasn't a single part of me that resented the authority emanating from her. That surprised me; I was pretty sure I spent all of this evening a moment away from throwing up all over this high-roller shit, but nope, nope, nope, India was exempt from the scorn I usually held.

"Probably not. I'm a stone heavier with hypocrisy and not just from this feast."

"Of course. But I should tell you why you are here..." She leaned forward and I watched her right hand go under the table. There was the faint sound of a button being pressed and a persistent whine just at the edge of hearing. I scratched at the inside of my ear and tried to yawn in case my ears had popped. She noticed and looked aghast. "You can *hear* that?"

I kept at the ear, making the sort of faces you do on your own and you're bored and you haven't put any outside clothes on. "Yeah what *is* that? It came on all of a sudden, but you're not going at your ear like a drill; what's your sundamned secret?"

"It's to stop anyone we don't want listening in." She'd regained her composure.

Really? "And what are we going to talk about that we don't want anyone listening in?" I mirrored her pose. Whatever could that be?

"Your Ultsurfing for one, Ele."

That got me right where I lived. Now I can't see my face, but I'm pretty sure I blanched and didn't do the high-roller thing where they're screaming inside with their faces all serene-like.

"Before you feign ignorance, Gunny has kidney medication that I own the patent for and his wife never talks about how he makes his money. And he makes more than he should. It didn't take long for my data miner to make the link."

I let out a breath and begged my voice to stay even. "So, now what?" Wait, didn't Gunny talk shit about his husband last pre-flight? Was he in one of those group marriages?

"You can relax; I'm not going to turn you in. That would be such a waste. Your times have been getting so much better recently." I—wha—Ho—I mean, she was right; they had been getting better, you bet they had, but *how in the Sun did she know that?*

Something else too. When she said 'my data miner', I could've sworn I saw her eyes flick away for a moment. Over my shoulder. At something. Maybe someone? I couldn't—wouldn't—look now; that would be too obvious. But maybe if she looked again, I could excuse myself to the bathroom. 'Think over' whatever corporate espionage or sophisticated scheme she was about to get me to do. And see what I think she was looking at. I needed to get her to look again.

"Um, thanks?" A compliment's still a compliment.

"You're welcome," she said entirely too lightly, and poured another glass of wine, "shame the rest of your team don't share your... talent."

"Say what?"

She either did an eye-roll that made her entire face

roll, or she had command of facial expressions I didn't understand. "Your team. They're not as good as you…"

I gritted my teeth. Half for the privacy whine and half at the insult. What did she know about our season? What we been going through? How hard we work, all the sundamned time, only to be screwed over by bad luck, another team jumping our game, stealing our splits, our times, my times. A soup of losses with tiny floating morsels of wins dotted around; trying to say that our shit didn't stink. That, maybe, really, it was gourmet and we just had to be sophisticated enough to taste it. Well, to the Sun with that. India Palmer: I might've known you since I was knee-high from the ground, but this India Palmer; nah, what do I owe *this* India Palmer?

"Don't talk shit about my team, India." A rustle on the tablecloth brought her eyes to the serrated knife I had in my fist, knuckles paling with the tension. Then she rolled them. This time I recognised it.

"I was complimenting you."

"By putting them down—"

"I don't see how, or why, that's a—"

"Why would you? You high-rollers are all the sundamned same. Don't care about anything but yourselves!"

"*Don't.*" She slammed her glass onto the table. Wine splashed us, the stem and foot broke into pieces; some I could see and some I couldn't. Despite the nag in my ear, I was glad for the privacy cage or everyone would've heard us. I wanted to risk a look to see if we'd drawn anybody's attention though I couldn't look away. India's eyes were boring holes into me. I couldn't tell if it was pride or fear or their bastard child, but one of them let me hold her gaze. "*Don't you fucking dare.* I don't care about anything else? Me? Tell me why I've spent my entire sundamned life devoted to making everyone else's better?"

"India, I–"

"Pawel's life expectancy was 44. He'll be 60 in a week." That was meant to mean something to me? India's eye-roll came back. Had a dancing partner of a frown. "Did you think Gunny was his *real* name, Elerie?"

Um, kinda...

"Oh, grow up." Her voice practically dripped venom. Shit, did I say that out loud? I dropped my eyes then. She'd let go of the glass, and I was watching a trail of the wine snake its way around the disturbed plates on the table. Another trail followed in its stream. Blood. She'd cut her hand.

"India, you're bleeding," I said more to the table than to her.

"I think the words you're looking for are 'I'm sorry', Elerie."

"Sun, they are. I'm sorry, India." I risked looking at her now. She was pouring another glass of wine with her bleeding hand. She put the bottle down, label smeared with her blood. Now she wiped her hand with the napkin from her lap. She looked less mad. She looked past me, somewhere, smiled and let out a soft laugh.

"Selena wouldn't want us to fight," she said finally, draining her glass and filled it again.

Selena, my older sister. Thinking about her had hurt so much that I hadn't for ages. She raised me more than my alleged mother ever did. I followed her around like any kid sister would. Selena and India were attached at the hip growing up. They'd babysit me and Tosin, India's brother I crushed on hard, back in the day. Sun, I hadn't thought of Tosin in years either. He didn't bat an eyelid when I chose my new name. When I told him how I really felt inside, and that the 'me' everyone thought they knew was a prison and needed to die, die, die. He even threw me a coming out party for the occasion. A wake, he called it. It's funny how much of my old life I'd left back on Earth. I loved Selena more than anything in the world, and it made everything about when she died that much harder. I never thought about what that had done to India till now. Ele, you fucking idiot. How could you accuse of India being like every other high-roller?

India was right, of course. Selena wouldn't like us fighting at all.

India had her slate on the table and was attending to the screen, middle finger jabbing at the haptic interface. I played with my hands a little. I didn't have the money for a slate. Every time I wanted to look up and say... something, her eyes were still down on the screen and the words stayed unspoken, and mostly unformed, in my head. It was a silence she felt comfortable in that I was uneasy about keeping. A whir shook me in my chair. The whine must've masked the drone's arrival. It busied itself with clearing the table of the plates we no longer needed. India kept at the slate and the drone fulfilled whatever she'd inputted. It deposited another bottle of wine and a new glass. It sucked up the shards of the broken one out of India's hands and sped off. India rubbed at her palm, and I wrinkled my nose at the smell of adhesive.

"I think you could make us both a lot of money. And stick the knife into those who deserve it." She broke the silence. Her voice brought me back into the room, to the table, to the conversation. That India knew about me. But how could *I* make *her* a lot of money?

"I don't understand." I hazarded honesty.

"You will, in time. But first things first." She drew her glass to her mouth and drank deeply. Long, dark hair falling behind her head tipped back, neck muscles working. It couldn't have been a toast because I hadn't agreed yet. Had I? Did I have a choice really? As she drew forward once more a shiny something was inside the glass and she offered it to me. Wait, was that a *flash drive?* Sun, I didn't know they were still being made, or used. India was could-buy-a-planet rich; what was she doing with such an old piece of shit? Shakily, my left hand met the top of the glass after some silent coaxing that was all in her eyes. Reaching for the new bottle of wine on the table, she stilled me with a gesture, once-torn palm patched up, and refilled the glass herself, the antique now afloat. It was maybe the size of half my pinky finger. I looked into India's eyes. Our gazes held for a few moments, the privacy device the only sound other than our breathing and the creaking of the seats. She offer-gestured again and sat back interlocking her fingers.

Oh. Fuck.

I'm leaning into my chair, and India's sat waiting, watching. I shifted my glance between the slowly-moving drive and her intent eyes. Oh. This was the toast. The moment where either I backed down, said thanks for dinner and everything but I want nothing to do with high-roller shit. Took my chances that she'd accept my refusal with grace, not ask to be paid back, or she'd get super pissed and there'd be police waiting for us outside Nox. Or I'd drink, be recruited by India, spared prison and allowed to live my life, albeit with a mission.

There was clearly nothing else for me to do.

I drank deep, slow, desperate to get as much wine to follow the flash drive down my throat. A moment of discomfort but sure enough, I worked hard to get it down. I looked into the glass and the light caught something else floating in the wine. It seemed attached to the drive. I understood now. The wine was egress, this thing was regress. The tab sat on my tongue: fruity from the wine and metallic from its makeup. My warmness towards India was slowly cooling. She started to applaud—slow, deliberate, condescending—and it made me want to gouge her eyes out in the worst type of way. Why do I feel like she owns me now?

India covered the last of the bill. "If you're going to keep a hold of that tab, I'd advise we eat nothing more here and you don't eat anything else until you take it out, unless…" She left her point hanging in the air as she stood and signalled for our booth to descend to a runway exit. The drifting didn't take long and the attendant could tell who owned which coat.

SWEATING IN MY apartment. Normal service resumed.

I sat legs akimbo in front of a movable fan, head down over a mixing bowl. A pool of spit had been swirling around as I rocked the bowl with my thighs. That tab, vitally important that it sat on my tongue from Nox in North Ombro to here, yeah that tab? Went right down my irresponsible throat, didn't it. Being drunk is not the best prep for some clandestine dealings. So here I am, tentatively gun fingering the back of my throat in the hopes I can retch the fucking thing out. Plan B was beside me. A packet of noodles that even emergency rations would beat. One of those down me I'd be seeking porcelain within minutes. India's voice was playing through my head: 'a lot of money and stick the knife…' over and over. Everybody's on board with making lots of money. I'm hardly swimming in it right—unless the 'it' is payments I owe Gunny on this place, and right now, my own sweat. I couldn't really imagine who my skills could stick the knife into either. Unless it was another team—

Could it be another team? She *did* know I Surfed right off the bat.

I started retching just thinking about it. My eyes watered under the stress and no clink of the flash drive as a reward just yet. I blinked the tears away to look at the noodle packet again. I shuddered and the future smell came on as strongly as if I'd already gone and done it. Real vomit splattered into the bowl. It took a few goes. Coming and going. All that fine food I'd eaten barely kept down more than half the evening. Served me right; swanning about an Ombro, eating high-roller food. Sure enough, when the sting in my throat subsided, I coughed the dregs away, and there was the damn thing. Sticking out as much as a piece of tech in a bowl full of sick would. I barefooted my way to the sink to tip the bowl. I rinsed it out, felt a filmy substance covering the flash drive—probably to protect from hitching a ride inside both India and me—and tore that off whilst remembering where I left my terminal last. Masking VPNs when looking at anything suspect hadn't gone out of fashion here on Aurin. I piggybacked on one set up by my tech wizard friend Jet. No, that's not their real name. They full-on gagged when I told them what I had. Demanded we got on video so they could see the flash drive for real.

They hadn't seen a working one since their first trip to the Science Museum. I hadn't seen one outside of vintage films. They proceeded to tell me that whatever I'd been given, the fact it was on here meant it was the most top secret of top-secret shit and that I better VPN. Oh Jet, you have trained your student well, and I am already VPN-ing. Next, they would tell me how to work it, because y'know, not a lot of tech these days was compatible with such a fossil. Also, there was no telling what complications such old tech would have interfacing with its descendants, they said. They were talking like the drive could be carrying ancient diseases—like crack the ice/amber and the fossil lets out trapped bacteria type of scenario—and it made me laugh, but they were being dead fucking serious. It wasn't worth the risk or the 'I told you so'. I dutifully followed Jet's further VPN instructions (they said not to use the usual and the new set would be easy to follow, but by the Sun, they were *not*) and hosted the flash drive in a virtual connection air gapped from anything and everything important in my life (also Jet's wisdom because my machine wasn't compatible with a hardwired connection, but with the right program, I could connect to it remotely) triggering an immediate prompt demanding I hook up a headset. High-rollers: think they own you or some shit. I sighed my way onto my feet and found my headset in the cupboard where my plates lived (what the fuck?) and sat back down, leaning my back against the one comfortable armchair in my living room, laid the computer on my lap, tied my hair into a bun, and connected the headset.

Now I know she's got money. And money lets you do all kinds of impossible stuff. But how did she get a hold of *this*?

I knew exactly what I was seeing the moment the first readings flashed up in front of me. Routes, trajectories, speeds, impact zone reads: it was the next game we were playing. Against the league leaders. This was their playbook, the whole thing, complete access to their formations, roster rotations, carving completion percentage, top speeds of their Speeds, I could go on. *It* went on and on. With this data, the Royals would really *eat* it! The point when my moral compass should prick me was feeling pretty blunt. I took off my headset and gave the noodle packet, once standing on its width's edge, my best punt across the room. I took my Minul to the wall terminal and ordered a raw fish platter. I was gonna be up all night memorising this shit and I needed to pack my brain full of that good brain food.

I COULD FEEL the bass in my skull, and it was a little annoying. But it was also exactly what I needed right now.

Polly came to my rescue during the all-night cramming and emotional beatdown I'd taken. She tells me that I need to come out. That the cloudchaser needs her 'hotshot' Speed. That she needs my support. That anything I was currently doing couldn't possibly be as important as coming to her aid. Could I have told her: no Polly, I can't come out; I'm sitting on the sunblessed jackpot of the year? My evening and maybe every evening till the game is gonna be full of impact zone formations and what the Royals' sign language gestures were? I thought about India, and the face she made throughout, and I couldn't imagine she'd enjoy her laundry being aired. And I know Polly and how she can never shut her sundamned mouth. So I rolled over. I probably should've stayed in, but I'm way too old for homework to keep me going out. Besides, I needed a minute. I wasn't going to beat the Royals tonight anyway. And my spirits needed lifting. A night out with Polly always helped.

I left everything—the headset, the laptop,—in my room but out of sight, because... I don't know why. Seemed rude to have it all just out in the open. I left the drive in the safe under my bed. I stood in front of one of the few fans still working and tried to dry out the jumpsuit for another journey outside. Polly sent me a ping, and I pulled it up to play whilst I looked for pit stains, back stains, chest stains. Polly wasn't alone. Ava was there, hands full of bottles, wearing a smile I didn't know she was capable of. I didn't know that Ava and Polly had even met. To most of the team, Polly's just a voice on comms. The whole plausible deniability thing. Like, we're not even meant to be friends outside of the games, but we thought to the Sun with that.

I sent a ping of my own—the state of my sweating, the concentration line that had begun forming on my forehead, the empty food packets—and signed it off asking who else was gonna be there, and what I could *possibly* help with. When the reply was more yelling and bottles and air kisses and pleas to come out, I gave up on trying to get an answer out of her. The video was also inconclusive to the party's attendees, but it didn't stop me hailing a taxi to Virtual Freeality. When the taxi came, it was one of those automated ones, and the silence was welcomed. We passed a checkpoint to one of the East Ombros, the line no shorter than the one I stood in hours ago to North, and I was glad to be going out with my own kind. Something told me there'd be another scheme at the end of this outing too...

The second I'd made it inside, Polly locked me in a fierce embrace and showered my face with kisses. When she pulled back, before I could even mouth a hello or a 'who's here?', she dug a hand into her bra and held a translucent strip to my face. I acquiesced, opening my mouth, and she pressed it into the roof of my inviting maw. I licked its length with my tongue; the sweet, slightly metallic tang sank onto my taste buds and everything got that bit brighter, sharper, louder, throbby, and more intense. Polly always had the best stuff. I poked a thumb at her mouth, and she shook her head and tapped her nose. Of course. Mixing was *never* a good idea. Hallucinatory shivering, crippling paranoia, and the desperate need to shed my mortal body to become part of the cosmic dust that makes us all and free my energy out, out, out wasn't a grand way to spend an evening. Polly left the embrace, still had me by the hand, and moved me through the throng of the downstairs room. A mixture of stationary and dancing people filled my vision and my senses. Every person that I weaved round, bumped into as the drug set in, or had to talk to negotiate around left an afterimage. Something ephemeral, residual to sit somewhere between my limbic system and my eternal soul.

We got to the bar. Still no sign of Ava or any of the party present on the ping. Polly rested her forearms on the bar and hunched forward to yell something in the bartender's ear, leaving me slightly to my own devices. I was a buoy, bobbing on the ocean waves, only peripherally aware of Polly's hand, my anchor, my tether to something and someone else. Nox and North Ombro were a storm on the horizon ever receding. The strip was magic. Bona fide witchcraft from the old world. How did I almost turn this down? Ugh. Strings tugged on my limbs, and I moved a little to the music, rocking Polly who was attempting to wrestle with a growing amount of glasses of drinks that the bartender was assembling. She turned to me, shot glass in hand. I swallowed hard. My heartbeat had moved four centimetres to the right. She took one look at my swallow, maybe saw something in my eyes, and she returned to the same pose with a different glass of a different, clearer liquid. I received the glass, its fragrance wafting to make my nose wrinkle. I licked the strip again, the energy release so instantaneous, so delicious, and sent the shot down the hatch. The back of my head hit something, and I gnashed my teeth together, narrowly missing my tongue. I whirled round ready to do bloody murder.

It was Ava. She was in another world. Literally, as I clocked the stimband wrapped around her eyes, her pupils saucers and darting around seeing whatever vid or simulation she was in. A moment of recognition settled on her face; the big smile and upturned face focussed on me. She held her hands prayer tight and apologised. Right to my ear and far too fucking loudly. She leaned back and was quickly sucked back into the stimband. The rest of the gang were around her I realised. How Polly got her to come out tonight, I don't know. But Polly could sell water to a fish. Some of the newbies from the team and other people I'd probably met before but had lost their names to the wind gently rocking my buoy. They one by one filed in to take glasses and an assortment of strips and vials from Polly. Jewellery, bracelets, chokers, piercings all lit up briefly in that all too familiar flash of totems interacting with their Minuls. *That's* why I didn't recognise most of them. They were Polly's *customers*, mixed in with her actual friends. A few of them dispersed back into the crowds. Ava remained with four others. They took the remaining glasses and deactivated their stimbands to make conversation.

No, you're Elerie, we've met before, you're introducing yourself again, but we know you. I'm Polly's roommate, I'm Polly's supplier, I'm Polly's best mate, I'm Ava's sister, I'm Ava. The words tumbled at me, sending lapping swells towards me, chiding, probing, but never in danger of sending me capsizing. Ava had a spare stimband and didn't wait for an invitation before pressing the buds in my ears. I heard a button, a few beeps, and I saw the band start to light up. Hands on my shoulders propelled me forward from the bar onto the dancefloor for real.

Soon the dancing around me began to fall away as the stimband booted up. Accessing my brain on fire. They were powered by your imagination; digitised your thoughts into avatars and images with near-perfect precision. So, with the strip, the shots, the vibe of tonight, oh I was in for it. And anyone who hitched a ride with me. The ocean filled my sight no matter where I looked. My body was the buoy. The buoy was my body. Giant craft adorned the seas, groaning, hooting at one another. Organic wails and artificial chimes. All lit up with revellers on the deck, waving to the buoy, to me. Smaller sea creatures pulled along the whales' stream, clinging to the blubber, feeding off each other in that ecosystem way that science loves. I wanted to wave back. I felt my body far away doing the waving to the music. The swell grew. A wave as tall as mountains formed. It was the entire world. My entire world. The buoy, me, pulled up its sheer height. I felt my stomach try to empty itself. I closed my anatomical eyes and the ocean winked out. When I reopened them I was somewhere else. On land. Not a storm in sight, thank the Sun. Ornate, high-ceilinged, full of people with masks. A mixture of high-rollers and the scum that I called my people. As they came into focus, there was Polly. I watched an asymmetrical dress bloom from the centre of her chest. Purple, tight and sleeveless across her right shoulder with a left sleeve that sat across her palm. She wore platform boots that made her taller than me. Her hair was knitted into this braid, with shorn sides, bleached almost white. She moved towards me. We were surrounded, but nobody had eyes for me but her. She took one of my hands in hers, placed the other on my hip, and led me around the ballroom with grace I stumbled to follow. At least it wasn't fucking ballet.

'I'm in love with Ava,' she said in a whisper.

I tried not to fall into the singularity her words had created at the edges of the room. Love. Ava. Polly. In love. What? 'D-does she know?' I asked.

'I don't know. You know how she is. Angry all the time. I think she'd hate the fact I've dated men in the past.'

'Huh.' My mouth and mind weren't doing a lot.

'And I don't *Surf*. I'm just the sky bitch to her. On the ground, incapable of flying. I'm a beetle and she's a bird of prey, one of her wingbeats and I'm dislodged from the mud, sent flying, antennae overloaded, fear receptors all ablaze, waiting for the moment I'm crushed under the weight. Disarticulated like something sad and dead.'

I hoped she didn't mind the silence. But, weren't you supposed to contemplate, introspect, *digest* poetry when you heard it anyway? The words descended an elaborate pulley system from my brain to my mouth. 'Does Ava deserve this poetic heart of yours?'

'Oh fuck you, Ele.'

'No, seriously. I've never heard you say anything like this about anyone and we've known each other for a long time.' I had; six long years. She was my squatting buddy, a mentor in activism and total hedonism at a time, post-mother ejection, when I was a bit lost. The steps of the dance, bless the Sun, got simpler and some of Polly's insistence on me coming out was starting to take root. Root, trees, forest. The edges of our ballroom grew gnarly, no longer burdened by the restrictions of architectural integrity. Windows shattered and were pulled out of their fixtures. Sunlight, dappled through thick branches, refracted from what glass remained from the incumbent nature's onslaught cast us all in rainbow splendour. 'Have you said anything to her?'

'That's why you're here.' She was smiling and her eyes behind the mask were shiny. From the light or maybe from tears I couldn't tell. The ceiling of our shared virtual reality had torn away completely. Thick leviathans of bark and branch started coiling around one another.

'You know *I* can't tell her how *you* feel. That's entirely your job.' I was laughing.

The Surf

She pouted and stuck her tongue at me. 'Sun, I know that. But you can help me take her to somewhere cool, though. I mean, look at what you've done to this place!' She leaned me back and held me there. My ballroom was an overgrown thicket, wild and untamed. All those dancers were moving flora, swaying towards wherever the sun broke through the canopy. Some of them moved in tandem with us.

Polly pulled me upright and the sensation lagged. My consciousness lingered in the previous position and reoriented itself inside me moments later. 'Not here; we should go somewhere else,' I said. Polly nodded and let me go. I pressed on the buds, keeping my eyes closed so I wouldn't have to watch the reality give way to *reality* reality. When the bass sent my ribcage thrumming, I reopened. I felt hot, and I fanned myself. Polly was sweating and looking around over my shoulder. No doubt trying to locate the love of her life. On the floor above where we stood were the private rooms. There they allowed for larger group sessions. Down here we could sync with anyone we sent invitations to. Hardly the easiest to declare your love in. I pointed up and rubbed my thumb against my first and middle fingers. With a grimace. Polly placed a hand on her chest and her face showed mock outrage.

First things first, though. Courage. We stood in a fast-moving queue for the restrooms and shared a cubicle. I put on my best Gunny impression and delivered a pep talk for the ages. My strip was running mostly dry, and I peeled it off the roof of my mouth. Ever seen magnesium go up in flames? That's what the strips do when they were sucked dry and you wanted to dispose of the evidence. Polly already had my replacement ready and waiting. She attended to her two lines of Sand first. She pressed it in, and I took her hands in mine and kissed all of her knuckles. Her pupils moved with the music, I swear. Maybe she was the closest thing I had to a best friend. I'd never told her that, but Sun, I hadn't really thought about it enough either. Shit, did I feel good!

Polly gathered our unruly horde and motioned that we all move upstairs. Ava had appeared beside her, and I watched Polly's hand linger on her arm as she told her the plan. My first bit of advice executed to perfection. Bellamy materialised next to me and put her around my shoulder and started saying something that was far too quiet under the music. My arm wove around her waist for ballast as we moved behind the pack. She led us as I looked around, and I swear I caught the eyes of someone staring dead at me. Weird. In a room of perpetual motion, this person stood alone, unmoving, with eyes that followed me through bodies and obstacles. Something about them seemed familiar. More of the strip dropped into my body, and with it fell away any chance of doing something about that feeling. Shaking off that sensation was paramount as ascending the stairs took more of my conscious attention than I would've cared to admit. We stood at the entrance to the private rooms. Stood, though, was an exaggeration. I was positively buzzing, shifting from one foot to the other, pulling Bellamy this way and that with me. She didn't complain. She said it was a lot like when we Surfed together, her in my slipstream. I smiled and felt a little tug of warmth

The Surf

in my stomach I put to the shot I'd just been handed and mainlined. Polly swiped her totem and the bouncer let us all through. The music died away and the lights were dimmed up here. A narrow corridor with rooms on either side, many of them engaged. Whatever revelry the rooms held, kept sacred by immaculate soundproofing. If I listened out for it, I was sure I could hear that same whine from India's privacy device. If I had ears for anything that wasn't either Bellamy's compliment speech or trying to listen in on Polly and Ava.

We were beckoned into a round room. There was a bin where we left our stimbands. A dispenser stood by that bin with new ones. I helped Bellamy with hers and she helped me with mine. With all the secrets I'd been told recently, I felt the need to unburden myself of mine, to share like the generosity I'd received. Before I could follow that through, our stimbands synchronised and we were transported to wherever whoever was leading. The floor and walls fell away. My jumpsuit was replaced with a flight suit I knew so well. I could almost feel the sun on me. The hot bluster of the Surf.

SPLIT ACTIVE IN 15. We were all pinged. The suit's HUD summoned as readily as in real life. I could see how we were divided. Into five pairs. Bellamy and me. That didn't seem like an accident. Geneva and Raine. Nina and Patch. Anne and Annie. Of course, Polly and Ava. Most of these names I missed or didn't remember earlier, but the syncing, the sunblessed syncing, made everyone's accessible. A privacy policy thing, I think. So you wouldn't have intruders in your session because, whoa, the things people get up to in here...

SPLIT ACTIVE IN 10. There was only one gate I could see. Right in the middle of all of us. The distance far exceeding the room we were in. Impact zones dotted across the sky. Smaller dots whizzed around as other teams took shape. Greys, Escorts, Slips. We were all Speeds.

SPLIT ACTIVE IN 5. I signed to Bellamy to lead and her helmet went transparent to send a smile back my way. A nice touch.

SPLIT ACTIVE. We kicked off and suddenly I was alone, suspended in the air. My body defied my every attempt to move. You try to do something nice for someone, and you always end up free-falling to certain death, huh. I watched the HUD indicate my accelerating heart rate and I cycled through every spiritual exercise I once mocked to try and calm myself down. To no avail. I looked down and saw the ground fast approaching. I gritted my teeth and prepared for impact. I touched down softly. Huh. In front of me stood the staring person from downstairs. They moved towards me gracefully, in a flight suit. They touched their helmet, and it did the same transparent trick Bellamy's did.

'You shouldn't be here,' the voice said, and I couldn't place it at all.

'Are you—where am—how are you doing this?' I shouted. I watched walls build up around us, the ceiling hurrying to knit itself closed, the night sky visible just before the two sides met.

'You shouldn't be here,' they said again as an interior began forming. The plane I stood upon raised itself from the ground, turning into blacks and silvers and reds of light fixtures, holo-paintings and tables and satellite booths.

Nox.

'Clever,' they remarked.

'You know India,' and an avatar of her sprung up on the other end of the table I was sat at. The flight suit disassembled, and in its place I was wearing the same dress as her. It fit, felt, like a second skin.

'And you know she won't appreciate you wasting your time here.'

'Oh really? And what do you know about what she wants?'

'More than you, clearly.'

'You high-rollers are all the same.' They'd sat beside India, and she started pouring them a drink.

They had shed the suit too and wore a tight jacket on top of a shirt buttoned only halfway up. Unnaturally green eyes set into a face both harsh and beautiful that was always changing. Everything save the eyes. For a second it rested on one, or did I pause it, and that's when the face made sense to me. The attendant at Nox. India's involuntary eye slip when she said 'data miner', the chance I never got to fulfil just hours ago. 'She told me you got that from her...'

'Got what?'

'High-roller, Elerie,' ugh of course they knew my name, 'India also convinced me that you'd be ready to play your part, but, now that I've met you, I don't know what she sees in you.'

'Don't think for a second, I'm gonna let you—'

'Go home, Elerie,' they said, interrupting me. I started

again and Nox was torn away. I was back in the sky. The game was done, Polly and Ava had won. The switch was so fast I felt disoriented. I threw up in my helmet and hoped I hadn't in my body too. I sat back and felt something solid under me. The stimband powered down, and Bellamy was crouched over me. Stroking my hair, keeping my head supported under her arm because it suddenly got too heavy for my neck. Like gravity had me in a lasso. An unruly mare. I hadn't thrown up, thank the Sun, but I had drooled kinda everywhere. She was the only one that seemed to notice. I looked over to Polly and Ava who were very preoccupied with trying to fall down each other's throats.

'Do you want to get out of here?' Bellamy asked.

'I need to go home,' I managed to get out.

'Here, I'll take you...'

Sounds in the kitchen invaded my dreamless sleep, and I woke up to a dry mouth and a comedown for the ages. My clothes were heaped at the foot of the bed. If I thought looking at them would resurrect memories of when and how I took them off, I was sadly mistaken. I rolled over to my bedside table and pulled open a drawer. I rooted around the innards till I got the pill bottle I needed. I worked my tongue in my mouth, and saliva did materialise, thank the Sun. I screwed open the lid and slipped two of the capsules into my mouth and lay back with my hands pressed on my eyes. Focussed on swallowing the pills that help me be me.

By the time I'd mustered the energy to prop myself on my pillows, Bellamy walked back into the room with two plates of breakfast. The slats on the windows let some of the light through, and the smoke and smell from the plates got me excited about the impending restoration of my human status. Bellamy wore a pair of my overalls that I forgot I still owned and she had her hair heaped onto a bun high on her head.

'You have a terrible diet, Ele.' She handed me the loot. Nothing on the plate had come from *my* fridge. On the plate was a bowl, and a red stew of vegetables and meat lightly bubbled within. Bellamy plopped herself beside me, nuzzled my shoulder a little, before handing me cutlery. We ate in mostly silence, shifting in the bed every now and then to keep our weight balanced. I didn't massively trust my internal buoyancy. Holding the plate, spearing food, chewing, all of these things seemed momentous to do at once. Slowly taste returned and I marvelled at the angel that was Bellamy and her cooking. When I say marvelled, that's nothing on when I watched her *bite* into the bowl. The crunch was satisfying and huh, what!

She beamed at me, 'try it.' I did and to the Sun, what artistry. A masterpiece. Was I still high? Because I'd never tasted anything so good homecooked. This was Ombro-level! A cheesy pastry of some kind. Mouth still full, I butchered the sounds of 'thank you' and didn't look to see in case any of it spat onto her or the bed with the effort. When we were done, she took the plates back into the kitchen, and I went to take a shower. Do I tell her what India's given me? Maybe it would help to have another partner in crime to achieve this plan. But I thought about India's face, and that annoying data miner who nagged, nagged, nagged at me. What we talked about, I couldn't remember, but I felt anger rise in my chest when I tried to.

I came out in my towel to an empty house and a note on my dresser. Bellamy was going to training. And she was taking my overalls as payment for last night. Bitch looked better in it as well. I checked my terminal and didn't see any training in my schedule. Hmm. With a free day looming before me, my mind went back to India and dinner. Tosin. How could I have forgotten to keep in contact with him? Okay, I resolved to find him, hit him up, meet him. Catch up on the years we'd missed that we could've shared. I'd apologise, swear to the Sun to be as good for him as he'd been for me. He'd forgive me; of course he would. So that's what I did. I sat at my terminal and went searching for him. Being the brother of one of the richest women in the system, I didn't think it would be too hard. But after at least an hour of sleuthing, I'd come up with nothing. Well, that was strange. Impossible, even. Where could he *be*? I took a deep dive into all the public records, articles, features and profiles on India and her company. Rehashed all the things that I knew. Again, no mention of Tosin. A previous marriage, charitable donations, her foray at turning producer in the film industry, a scathing op-ed from one fucking misogynist journalist creating a dating profile for the system's most eligible 'bitch'.

This made no sense. They'd applied for resettlement a couple years before we did, and her family, well, they didn't just fit the criteria, they *were* the criteria! Maybe my birth parent would know? My finger hovered over my last known number for her. That's all it did, though. Nothing would make me call that woman again.

Now I was strapped to a breather, pads attached to my chest, a real-time projection of my vitals as my running mate. Mostly real-time. The projection was running harder than me, *beating* me. It had been almost half an hour, and she'd opened at least a two-hundred metre lead on me. Sun! It had been a couple days since I'd trained. Well, I was doing *something*. Cerebral things, for the last two days. Training the mind, y'know? The Royal hand-signal language was deep. Us Tadpoles stuck to the basics, how to communicate with other members of the team and relay vital information to one another. The Royals. Well, shit. They could talk about the search for the meaning of life, that's how deep they'd gone. Fusing real sign language with an adapted gestured alphabet, it conjured the image of them doing just that. Their Speeds talking about the latest vids everyone was watching, how long to sauté ingredients for a fancy dish, Sun, even the repatriation of the indigenous people that used to call Aurin their home. Back when they called Aurin something entirely different. I wouldn't put it past them. My legs pumped faster, my motion tensed and I watched the metre count tick down and down. My avatar looked beside/behind her at me. She smiled.

"Wherever this gear came from, keep it up, Ele," she ordered, "that's it, push, push! Don't let me beat you again!" And I ran and ran. Tuning out the avatar's encouragement and lap time updates. It was just my lungs burning and my anger at the Royals. It took me ages to realise that the treadmill had stopped beneath me. I shook myself back into my body and eased myself into a cooldown walk. My avatar had long since disappeared. I looked at the time on the monitor. Of course she'd still beaten me... It made me laugh anyway. It was nice to be back out in the world. Other Tadpoles were going through their routines on the different equipment across the two levels of the complex. All striving for personal development and an uptick in our team's fortunes. Gunny sat in an office in the back with a few of his staff watching film. They would pause, switch angles, flight suit perspective, team plane overview, analytics overlaying each image with numbers and graphs and icons. I took a seat at the back of the room, mopping at my sweaty self, and tried not to disturb them. Onscreen was our last fight with the Royals. I say 'fight' because it was a bloodbath.

Ultsurf is essentially one big time trialled relay race. There are six splits in a hexagon that the teams must navigate through in an order dictated by the gamemaster.

And since it's a race, the faster time your team records a split, the better. Speeds, like me, score the most points from split to split. The team that gets all their Speeds through a split first or record the single fastest time 'own' it. Eight Speeds per team meant eight chances each to clock that fastest time while the split is active. When the next one is called out, that's it, your scores are final and it's not like you can go back. We were Surfing against two other teams. Three splits down: we had one, the Jackals one, and the Phalanx owned one and were closing in on the fourth. The Phalanx were the city's other team and our nearest, dearest rivals. Last season, James the Lesser was on the Phalanx. He joined us this off-season. A fact no one would let him forget. It's how he got his name. He's bigger, stronger, older, and *better* than our James, but he was dubbed James the Lesser first practice and that was it. If he had any hard feelings about it, they didn't show.

Anyway, this was a game we felt good about maybe winning. The Phalanx switched up their playbook after we'd acquired Lesser, of course, but he and Gunny together were a terrible twosome. Able to anticipate *what* changes they might make, and how we could counter their formations. The Phalanx might have been closing in on the fourth split, but our Slip team controlled a lot of the impact zones on the way and put us in a sunblessed position to take it and the lead.

Then the fucking Royals.

So, since the sky is everywhere, there are a lot of games that play simultaneously. The interference we run to try and throw the authorities off us, is also designed to throw *other teams* off. See, there's no rule saying how many teams can play in one game. When game areas are pinged, you scramble to the location and as long as two teams are there at the start, then the Surf's up. Cloudchasers like Polly and team leaders like Gunny, it's their jobs to find the nearest game, throw our signal all over the place so if you looked at a game, and saw it was overcrowded, teams would look elsewhere. There were only so many splits to go around after all, and six is a small number to divide more than three. The signal barrage worked as a big-time bluff and also meant in your path to a game, it was advantageous to see what other games you could get to along the way, what splits you could steal for extra points. The Royals were the *best* at stealing splits. Their Speeds claimed split four before we even knew they were in the game. They further announced their presence with their Greys chewing out so many players for the remaining splits. Our team was deep into our rotation of players with so many down for the count during play, and I'd got more airtime than in any other game in the season so far. It was when I stopped giving Lesser shit. He was *pissed* that we were losing, to the Royals *and* our chance to give it to his old crew. The Royals took the final two splits winning the game three to one to one to one. Our combined times put us *just* above the Phalanx, so we'd beaten *them,* but who honestly cares enough about first loser to be happy with second?

You know, we spend so long scared of the nightmare that the Royals would swoop in to steal splits that I don't think anyone had ever done it to them. No matter how much we all wanted to. Evolution in all its glory. Prey remains prey.

A trainer brought my flight suit right before the film session ended and it was time to get into the air. To put some of whatever they'd tactically adjusted into practice ahead of the big game. For hours. Every single day. Training games were the only time we were up in the plane without one of Gunny's speeches. It was mostly comms with your squad leader and co-ordinator, but before we bottomed out, I pinged Gunny directly. I asked him if he knew anything about why people, sometimes, didn't want to be found. He'd paused, and here was me waiting, thinking like he'd give me some old-timer insight into the world, but all he said was if I didn't wanna find myself on a team, I should ask him again. As if he'd ever take me seriously. I felt like the biggest idiot and my seat dropped me out of the plane into the warm embrace of today's sky.

I HAD TWO projects now. And one obstacle to navigate.

Though I wish I could Surf for a living, insurance underwriting paid my bills. My official job. My company had been given a whole project funded by the government. There was a new planetary defence array slated to be put into construction, and infrastructure needed to find land, jobs, planning permissions, and greenlit. We were being 'encouraged to pull' overtime to get all the paperwork in place for the high-rollers. There were conversations that people at the office who talked to other people at the same office had with each other that I tried not listening to but couldn't help overhearing. About politics. About diplomatic relations between Aurin's nations and how a defence array was meant to work as a great deterrent for global unrest. A great way to find out there was global unrest in the first place! Instead, it could serve as a momentum to a continued cooperation between all of us on our new home; to avoid the mistakes of the past. Okay, shut up, maybe I was eavesdropping. Once, an aptitude test outlined a multitasking deficiency in me, but here I was insuring millions of credits of hardware, software, and real estate, with a double life thought stream dedicated to beating the Royals, and not to mention time away from both of those *jobs* spent looking in the archives across the city that contained all the data on the Aurin resettlement program. Three jobs. If that woman, my mother, could see me now! All the doubters could all take their static evaluation of me, their disappointment, and their doubt, and their pity, and go off-world with it because that was the *only* place the Sun didn't fucking shine!

Despite being public record, there wasn't a great amount of information available. One of these nights I found myself at Jet's, and they wouldn't budge with their clearance, the spoilsport. I said, not even for the joy of seeing a flash drive, and they told me, in between submission holds as we worked out, that morality and professionalism for people not called Elerie Astrada wasn't an opt-in/opt-out type of affair.

I couldn't hold an armbar on them long enough to alter their decision-making at all. Ugh.

I was on my own with this one. India didn't contact me at all. Maybe she didn't want to talk about Tosin. Maybe something happened between them, like me and the womb I escaped, and they didn't speak anymore. I was hardly her confidante, so I couldn't ask her, could I? There was a point when I thought maybe I'd hallucinated everything: the dinner, the meeting, the plot. Okay, several of these points, but every time I went home and hooked the headset up, the Royals were naked right before my eyes, and I stopped trying to doubt my reality.

OH YOU HAVE got to be sundamned kidding me...

Now I've never felt like the most creative person, and I sure as shit didn't prescribe to this notion that 'inspiration' strikes you and you become this possessed conduit of pure, raw creation.

But that's the only way I can describe how I feel at this present moment. Mid-wipe, practically forgetting how to do the rest of the process I sat down to do in the first place.

Jonah and the Aurin Audit.

His 'art', once a target for my castigation, I would turn to in my time of need. First: the art. Failing that, I would seek the artist. As the toilet flushed, I sorted through discarded clothes in my room for my headset. It would be a much quicker process than using the laptop. And predictably enough, it was bound up with my flight suit's underlay. Also completely spent of juice. And who knows how long I could ride this inspiration wave! Laptop it was. I took my totem from its resting place around my left wrist and pinned my hair back from my face with it. I put the headset on its charging station and lamented not owning the model that could simultaneously charge *and* run. If *I* could multitask, so should something this sundamned expensive. I looked through the trash of my Minul's data storage first. Because knowing me, any of the Audit would've ended up in there. My search turned up nothing. Maybe I hadn't deleted them? I combed through logs close to our relocation and in the few years shortly after. More nothing. He *did* say his content was confiscated; maybe he wasn't full of shit? I pulled up the net, and searched for Jonah himself. There he was and not a single aspect of him had changed. A self-styled media mogul, a defender of truth and free speech, ironclad in his crusade to answer every 'why' there was. Positive testimonies from clients, staff employees and employers alike littered his site. Half of them even seemed real. I never knew which one came first; if the Audit inspired Jonah to take on this mantle or the other way around. I want to say for as long as I've known him he's been this way, but there's definitely a time when I didn't know him super well and I was way more concerned with trying to get to know myself.

The site autoplayed a hologram of Jonah. His projection seemingly took stock of its surroundings from the screen. Without ceremony or a whiff of consent, Jonahgram stepped out of the back of my laptop, projected via a feature I had no idea it possessed. The likeness was uncanny, and it did sure look like there was *weight* to the digital intruder. He paid greater attention to the room I was in, and I felt self-conscious at the appraisal. Would his pixelated fingers swipe dust from surfaces? Would the dust be pixels or corporeal motes? Thank the Sun he did none of those things. He just proselytised, instead. Presumably on a script written for my IP location, server ping, and speed of my processor. Jonahgram was forensic in its categorising my quality of life and listed options at different subscription packages 'well within my financial means' I could sign on to maximise my 'potential'. Serving grandiloquence of the highest order.

'Are you not swayed by stats from 'experts'?' Jonahgram asked me, complete with bunny ears around experts.

'No, Jonah, I hate stats,' I answered.

'Of course you hate stats. I bet you're like me. Raw data is incomprehensible without context, without the human touch of understanding. So please, allow some of my friends to let you know how they benefited from this program.' He beckoned a lineup of holograms behind him. A *diverse* gang of people, similarly unbound by the dimensions of my laptop screen, with headlines hovering above their heads. Buzzwords like 'intimacy issues', 'substance abuse', 'imposter syndrome' and 'body dysmorphia' emanated from the roster of the hopeless, of the lives turned around, and I wondered whether the images were them before or after their transformations. Not being able to tell the difference seemed counterproductive to the messaging. I sat through what seemed to be the same story run through differing filters of sadness and misery. I yawned and was ready to leave Jonah and his cult of personality after suffering through the latest borefest when—

'Wait, go back,' I said. When they continued, I demanded it pause and rewind. Idiot, it's not one of those programs. I mashed the keyboard buttons, so the sob story started again. Readjustment problems were the focus of this person's malaise, their visage was giving androgynous in a way that had me looking on with serious envy eyes, and as I listened and relistened to their script over and over, it seemed vague. *Infuriatingly* so. That it made me want to drop it and not follow—

Jonah, I take it back, you are an *artiste*.

I can't believe I didn't recognise the traits. I mean, that was the point, but still.

In what was either a hack move or my dream of having a cipher with another human being, this anatomical depiction of code was called Anderr.

A quick rearrange of the letters and you get 'Renard'.

And not what I thought was a glaring mistake that made it past too many levels of approval.

I LEFT 'ANDERR' mute, mid pace, in the middle of my living room as I retrieved a stylus and put on my spex. I played through the story again, and scrawled notes on what I thought were the dead giveaways of *some* kind of code. What do you get when you have a bunch of amateurs playing at tradecraft? You guessed it: nothing. Not a single sundamned thing happened. No secret message played, congratulating me, Elerie, on finding this trove of information, on inheriting the fight that he started, that *we* would finish. And to tell you the truth, that *sucked*. After India parachuted into my life to recruit me for one mission, I think I'd got a little drunk on being needed. That I could have some greater purpose, play a role in big events. Not today. All I got was an invitation to some bleeding hearts club; some support group that would help people with Anderr's problem, and it didn't come with any financial outlay at the start. The only thing it cost was time because 'an open mind is always free'... *ha ha Jonah*. There was a meeting in two days' time and I signed up for it.

'Thank you so much.' Anderr receded from sight and sound and Jonah came back, walking forward in a gesture so earnest, I marvelled at the coder who one and zeroed his wet eyes. 'For giving us the gift of your time and heart, please take this from me.' He held out a box, and I got a prompt asking if I wanted to accept the data transfer. I held my hand out as Jonah got closer and sure enough, that was the consent it needed to initiate. It remained in my hand, a gold cube that winked out of existence the moment it completed. 'It's timelocked to two days from now. For you, it will open doors.' And he left me with an optional survey to fill out for more Jonah-branded content.

I did not fill it in.

Elerie
Psst
Psst Ingrid

Ingrid
No one can hear u Ele

Elerie
Shut up
Don't be _that guy_ing
Ugh formatting
that guy

Ingrid
What do you want?

The Surf

Elerie
Can I not talk to my favourite colleague?

Ingrid
I am *not* your favourite
Do
Not

Elerie
What do you mean?

Ingrid
Lie
To

Elerie
I promise you aren't

Ingrid
Me
Wow

Elerie
*are, fuck ARE
I swear that was a typo

Ingrid
Fingers don't lie Ele and
your digits just typed out
some truth
I am *ending* this conversation

                        Elerie
                No wait pls I swear I didn't
            mean it it was a typo I swear
                    You're so dramatic

Ingrid
And unlike you I actually do
work here. I have a project
deadline coming up
Shareholders to appease

                        Elerie
                    I'll be quick then

Ingrid
You better be

                        Elerie
                How, like, old are you?

Ingrid
Huh?

                        Elerie
              I can't type it any louder

Ingrid
...haha

Elerie
No wait, HOW, LIKE, OLD
ARE YOU?

Ingrid
Wtf
Why Ele?

Elerie
Y'know, I'm curious

Ingrid
Want to know if u broke any
laws u old crusty?

Elerie
Fuck youuuu, I am *not* old

Ingrid
Admitting you're crusty tho

Elerie
No I'm not

Ingrid
Law of omission, look at
what you denied

> **Elerie**
> Grrrr...

Ingrid
Aw cute, did you make the
noise too?

> **Elerie**
> ...no

Ingrid
Don't lie

> **Elerie**
> Maybe idk yes
> Shut up
> Just answer the question

Ingrid
Not till you tell me why

> **Elerie**
> Okay fine lemme rephrase
> Were you born *here* or did
> you *move* here?

Ingrid
Here?

> **Elerie**
> Yeah here

Ingrid
Here like work?

                              Elerie
                     No! like *here*. Aurin.

Ingrid
Where is this going? Why are you asking me? Why is this important to you?

                              Elerie
                 Curiosity I promise. A project I'm working on. Nothing big. Cross my heart

Ingrid
Wait, ur not of *those people*, are you?

                              Elerie
                             SUN NO

Ingrid
Because I am going to have to rethink my decisions
And find out if you can *un*fuck somebody

                              Elerie
                              Harsh

Ingrid
But true

Elerie
Wait, I can't even do it like that

Ingrid
From what I remember, u couldn't do it at all...

Elerie
...
Seriously?
Wow

Elerie

> and find out if you can *un*fuck somebody

I meant *this*, you child! And I can do it just fine, ask around. Ask about me Ing. See what you hear

Ingrid
What? Find out about who else has been there? No thank you

The Surf

Elerie
Now that you've suitably
humiliated me and I feel
about three inches tall,
can you please answer my
question? Pretty please.
Then you can get back
to your super important
project and I'll find out if we
can unfuck

Ingrid
Cool I'll put something
in the diary and ur gonna
present your findings to me

Elerie
Scheduling... so sexy...

Ingrid
You know me. love an
organism

Elerie
Organism is already a word

Ingrid
Sun

Elerie
It's never gonna catch on

Ingrid
It will

                        Elerie
                Have fun explaining it every
                        time you say it
                          ANYWAY

Ingrid
Like you have to explain
high-roller every
sundamned time

                        Elerie
                        WE DIGRESS
                You were about to tell me
                  about where you were
                    ejected from your birth
                            prison

Ingrid
Was i?

                        Elerie
                        C'mon

Ingrid
I feel weird talking about
this
But I was born here

The Surf

Elerie
THANK YOU

Ingrid
WERE YOU?

Elerie
No I wasn't
K

Ingrid
Oh u weren't?
Wow u *are* old.
Like real old

Elerie
Don't make me come over there

Ingrid
I'd like to see u try
It's a whole lotta floors you gotta walk up
I reckon you'd get lost
Up here where the people matter

Elerie
Wow
Again
Just wow
Despite the *shade* you've been dealing today I'm gonna go easy on you this time
But know that I will be seeking my revenge
And when u least expect it
I
Will
Strike
With a vengeance
So till then, live in fear.
Otherwise
K get back to ur project u busy little thing

Ingrid
Oh thank u
I'm so scared
Drinks later?

Elerie
Let me check my diary

Ingrid
Fuck you

Elerie
Love you byeeeeeee!
xxxxxxxxx

INGRID WAS A 'Did we? Have we?' person last year. The night was super blurry and had plenty blank spots that I had done a deep intelligence gathering operation that only managed to collage vague pieces together. I say 'deep' but... There'd been a vibe since I moved into her team. At an off-site designed to deepen team bonds and effective delegation of duties, she and I got very close during an online scavenger hunt. With the spark now set, a few months later we were staying in a cabin out in what I can only describe as a giant terrarium. A closed-system biome project that was dangerously close to the kind of work my mother's new paramour specialised in. Then standing in front of a program for the event, I was confronted by his image without so much as a warning and my anxiety absolutely peaked. They were looking to resequence new flora, give evolution performance-enhancing drugs, to adapt to the sun sun sun of Aurin, so we could start moving towards eating food that wasn't grown in a lab somewhere, or hadn't been slowly thawed from the world's biggest drive-in freezer at CryoCore.

The most unique *mise en place* in human history, and we wanted rid of it as soon as possible. This was why we could never have nice things.

Did we trade with the people who were here before us? Learn how they did what they did? Like fuck we did.

So now it was the brute force gambit for us once again. History is a class and we keep being bad students. So my company, Fortified Solutions, and about twenty other clones of us had descended on this conference looking to secure the lucrative contracts up for grabs. Landing the defence array had elevated us to the big leagues, but it also attracted a lot of wide eyes and big noses. Looking for shit that smelt like shit.

Our bosses briefed us on our strategy. It amounted to never being caught on your own. To effectively partner with a senior figure so anyone looking to catch us with our pants round our ankles would find us with a second pair of safety pants. And leave with nothing but the sight of our tighty-whiteys. I was convinced our lives were going to be forensically mined, and potential liabilities left behind, but here I was swimming in water so clear you could see everything, foraging for food like I used to on Earth's wilds, cooking it out all natural over fires and sleeping in yurts with no need for air-conditioning.

Polly told me there was no way I was gonna get anything out of the trip sober with the impending threat of bumping into the gene wizard and his familiar, and she was right, as she generally was. I originally thought gene wizard was, like, a joke. Like if someone held a gun to your head and asked you to explain a job you had not a single clue of what they did. So you made shit up just to live. But no, it was his *actual*, sundamned title and I tried to imagine being that conceited. After the revelation, I had to get high, and fast, and with a second to stop any kind of emotional suicide ideation surfacing, and I'd convinced Ingrid to join me one night.

The Surf

She accepted the role with the appropriate severity but went halves on the pills I offered. We ran hand in hand on the expo grounds. Vast as they were under the domes. Interconnected and divided into the specialised villages. We had exhibitor clearance that allowed to access most of the site, but some of the more interesting niches of the expo were reserved for a privileged few. You couldn't help but think in those exclusive areas the real work was done, and out here, us normals played at the kids' table when the adults got together at their own with no invitations handed out.

But when a site steward politely asked Ingrid to get down from a solar system display unless we wanted him to call security, and gritted his way through her belligerence, I thought maybe the distinction was maybe quite useful. We found our way to a viewing deck and tried our sundamned best not to disturb anyone else. Our hyperventilating to their breathing. And we could've succeeded if it wasn't for Ingrid's slate. The thing buzzed like crazy. An alert for something she was meant to do. I had to turn it off because I had it in my hand. Wasn't the easiest task for my dismantled attention span, but I managed it without any further casualties to the ambience. That's when she told about the 'organism' idea. In giggled hush-hush talk. In more like a stage whisper, if I remembered correctly. She put in time for herself to get off, anything from five minutes to an hour. I told her that she couldn't possibly defy her schedule. And she looked at me. And I looked at her. Then we had to start the next project. And then something else. A haze, plenty of people, a keynote speech, a bonfire of dancing. A strong sensation of *release*. The events come back in flashes, in no particular order.

She maintains that 'we did' and 'we have,' and I've been taking her word for it ever since. She liked to bring it up if I ever did something not-so-great, and I wasn't in possession of enough information to dispute her. A lovely, pseudo-toxic power play dynamic that maybe I liked a little bit...

Ingrid wasn't an easy person to say no to, but I managed to avoid going to drinks with her and the others. There was a tentatively poised moment when she demanded to know what possible reason I could have for not attending this golden social gathering, and I was internally shouting *obfuscate* so heavily that I just stared at her. Eyes boring holes into her as she waited impatiently for an answer. She made a face—and not a cute one—and I had to go back to the drawing board fast and deliver an inscrutable exit strategy.

I settled on Renard.

She was nothing but thoughts, considerations, prayers, and assured me that intentions would be burned for my aura. She'd left me pings reminding me how strong a woman I was, that I wasn't alone, and that she could be trusted with any information in confidence. I put my phone in stasis, like the sign outside the group's door suggested, and knew, when I resurfaced, the supportive Ingrid-fest would have a sizeable encore. Renard was a card to play in any situation where you needed to be vaguely bleak enough that no one would dare cross-examine you. A family bereavement was an ongoing lie, one that required fuel, specificity, and an adherence to the relevant stages of grief. It had to live so you could. And I don't know anyone who's got the time and memory for all that. Renard, in all their glory, was the go-bag you needed. A gender non-specified vagrant in desperate need of saving; ostracised and all but given up on. Nevertheless you persisted, out of an indentured obligation from a non-specified event in your past, when you were Renard, and Renard was your lifeline back then.

With that being said, Renard's efficacy was in the imagination of the mark. A litany of possibilities would've formed in Ingrid's mind and her response to the gambit reflected how serious she'd gone for the only possible scenario that could tear me away from her social offering. And the alchemy necessary for turning Renard into a *pas de deux* would be in the next time I saw Ingrid. If she never asked about them. She could squeeze my hand if we were in a lift together as long as nobody saw. Allow more than just a greeting to pass between us through the medium of a nod. But to *speak* of Renard would break the spell, severing our nascent deeper *yet* wordless bond, too fragile to breathe for itself, or stand upon its vestigial limbs.

I couldn't believe that this usage of Renard was actually kinda true. If only Tosin were here, he'd be laughing at the chances; like this was proof that Jonah legit was a savant and I gave him a hard time because I didn't possess—what did he say back then? The *atoms*. That was it. Never one to back down from a self-oop, he said my number would be 0 because I was so periodically dumb it was basically constant, and I told him to avoid attempting chemistry-based comedy in the future if he ever wanted to get laid.

BACK IN THE present, I was trading my outer borough of Aurora for another. Today I had a date with some down and outs; my people. Though a different vintage fermented by a vintner I hadn't seen in years. Instead of hopping on another monorail from the office, I'd exhumed my electric bike from the modern art piece it'd formed among my detritus and did the forty-minute cycle into work. When I sent the location of later to my spex though, oh I was full of regret. I had over an hour to pedal from work. And that didn't take into account getting back home.

If only Pawel could see me now. The *cardio* I was about to put myself through.

Humidity was quite high today, low sixties my spex told me, and I was glad of the loose vest I'd worn today. My bike shorts hadn't seen the light of day for a lil' while, and they weren't as tight as they used to be. Hmm. Funny that. I triggered the route-finding and pushed off into the road when there was a break in the cars. Eased myself into the commuting peloton at a steady pace. Aurora's not an old city, not like Earth-old, and it's always something to remember when you're out and about. Real estate is still being auctioned and partitioned off with the potential for tenants, both residential and commercial. Once I'd signalled my way onto the cycleway out of the city centre, I watched buildings lose storeys and altitude for scaffolded skeletons and holoprojections of the promises to come. Drones whirred overhead pulling hours that human contractors didn't fancy themselves physically. Controllers oversaw their functions, an occupation you could do remotely, joysticks in front of a screen if you were low-grade, a VR setup with movements keyed to your muscles and a haptic interface for the fancier.

Jet, when they were being their government named identity, helped in the fabrication process of our synthetic helpers. Obsessed with birds, their design for the drones was based on how flocks of birds communicate, move, and coexist in harmony and synchronisation. The R&D was mostly under patent law, but occasionally Jet ran virtual simulations in the auditorium they had masquerading as their lounge. Damn—I wanted their salary, but I didn't want their hours. That simulation, though, it was incredible to watch. They walked amongst it with a stylus in their left hand, slate in the right, and I thought they looked like a real-life artist. They'd draw something on one of their pixelated creations, tap tap tap on the slate, a great big thing that must've been on the company payroll, their fix would reconfigure in seconds and the drone-birds would move to the adapted algorithm they'd implemented. They answered a couple of my dumb questions as they worked. They held one of the drone-birds in their hands and let me turn it over to see the design, before asking me for hush as they had some hard data to crunch and numbers to get to a presentable state.

As traffic backed up a little, I paused to snap a few pictures with my spex and dictated a ping to send over to them. As I kicked back into gear and rhythm a few minutes later, Jet's answer came back. They were all thanks but started going into upcoming code patches they were writing. Carried away with their work, they stopped, realised who they were talking to, and said they'd just see me soon. For dinner, or we'd catch a vid sometime. So cute. Name a time and place after this week I sent back; I couldn't go into *why* I was so busy—beating the Royals, beating the Royals, beating the Royals—of course, but Jet was a patient human, keeping their inquisitive, analytical mind at the door when it came to the cryptic currency of my calendar.

My spex told me I'd entered the borough of Blomqvist. Proto-borough was probably more accurate. Some stats popped up as I slowed my heart and pedal rate so I could sweat a bit less. A few months ago, it was an alphanumerical designation closer to a self-regulating password than somewhere people were going to live. As settlement began, there was a breaking ground of sorts and some of those pioneering folks conducted a survey for what the borough was going to be called. The alderman of A2H-D76-whatever and her assembled constituency agreed on Blomqvist, and the left turn I'd just missed meant the trivia was too engrossing for travel. I blinked the HUD away and powerslid into my 180 with expertise I wished an audience more than me could see. I turned right down the correct road and looked either side for my meeting location. I didn't have to look for long as I saw a few people milling outside smoking. I pulled up slightly past them, each side surveying the other, and proceeded to shut my bike down.

The Surf

I kicked at the ground as I walked back to the smokers and leant against the wall, not close enough to greet and not far away enough to be rude, while deciding my fingernails were the most interesting revelation for miles. The technique worked; the smokers took the hint, finished their work and walked in without interacting with me. I let the door shut and got to 1184 before I stopped multiplying 37 in my head. Nope, not enough time had passed yet, and I was so close to the square. 1369. Right, here we go, here we sundamned go. My hand slapped the flat of the door where the handle once was. Huh? Double take. Let me try again. Nope, nothing, no handle, no fucking handle. Exhale, think. You watched them go in. They probably don't want just anybody from the street walking in. Support groups lived and died by their anonymity and the security that created blah blah blah. It'll be why they chose Blomqvist in the first place. *Of course*! I smacked my forehead. That data packet Jonahgram handed me at the end of his spiel. I flicked the hairband on my wrist and after a quick scroll through my received items, I found it and I held that gold cube in my left hand.

Wait, is this gonna—

'For you it will open doors,' he said.

I held the cube against where the handle once was.

No, this is stupid, it couldn't poss—

The cube fused with the door. The gold dissolved into transparency and there was the image of the handle. It grew opaque and I glanced over each shoulder just to clock if anyone else was getting this. Inching my middle finger towards it, mid-wince, I let out a breath I had no idea I'd held when it met resistance. The handle must've 3D printed right there and then. Again, Jonah being so sundamned extra. If I saw him tonight, I'd hit him. He'd catch these hands, no doubt.

I turned the nascent handle and heard a 'Welcome Elerie' as I walked towards a descending stairway. The light wasn't great and every step was a gamble I made not to just walk off the face of the earth if the floor hadn't been put in. I could see arrows on the walls, all pointing down at intermittent intervals. Hand-sprayed arrows and not strip lighting like I'd suspected. I kept my chin tucked into my neck so I wouldn't give in to my urge to straighten up and hit my head on the low ceiling for my trouble. There was a D3 next to an open door. I flipped open my compact mirror. I dusted my cheeks in the low light and stuck one of Polly's strips on the roof of my mouth. It would eventually slow release micro dose if I didn't give it an activation lick straight up. Y'know, just in case this place, these people, do my head in. Walking through that open door I could taste the faint leftover smoke of those outside. I was going the right way. I just had to follow my nose now.

And the melody that had snuck into my ears. I'd been tapping my index finger against my thigh, nodding along unconsciously. It was singular and it was compelling. It bore under my breastbone, my ribcage, and lodged itself somewhere behind my left ventricle. I scratched at the place on my chest, and it tingled slightly. Voices joined the melody. Well, less joined, but more appeared. They were conversational, overlapping, markedly not in step with the melody, and as I rounded one more corner,

The Surf

I came to an atrium. In the centre of the room were chairs, pairs facing each other, one rested in the middle of them all. Light streamed down onto the seating area, and I began to make out the assembled others who all skirted the light and engaged in talking with each other. No sign of Jonah, though, yet. I'd give it time. I picked up a flyer, skimmed its words as I jammed it into my back pocket. A goofy smile for another who made eye contact with me. Shifty, incredibly fleeting eye contact, I might add.

Pretty soon the disparate rabble all moved towards the light, pairing off to take seats. Anxious not to get someone, I thought maybe that seat dead in the middle wouldn't get a partner—actually its prominent position would provide it, thus me, probably *more* attention. I course corrected a third time, aiming for a seat on the outside rows. Yes, this was better. Now under the lights, tonight had brought all kinds of people. There were gym dudes, pink, veiny, looking at risk of a pinprick or splinter to deflate them. The all comfort, zero style, spiritualist next to their recycled, blocky uniform fashioned trendy twin. Some suits that could've been high-rollers, and two people who chose the seat nearest that prime one who legit gave off that high-roller energy. The music increased in volume, adding a drone that pulled at my body towards the source of the sound. A gently padding, barefoot creature with a shock of orange hair, defying gravity to stand so vertically. Chains connected xir earrings to two nose rings. A top-heavy robe, all sleeves and barely anything beneath the waist, in golds and green. Floating beneath xir hands, an illumined lap steel guitar, that glowed when it was pressed rather than plucked or played. Xe did two slow circuits of us all; taking xir time to regard each person. To play for them, at them, then moving onto the next. Reactions differed, but at least everyone showed some respect, a bowed head, a fist bump, a strange handshake that saw one of the suits touch as high as xir inner bicep, and xe on him as their foreheads met. My tongue curled towards the strip. Could I risk it now? Xe held me in a gaze so welcoming first time around, I bade my tongue stand down, and by the time the return journey was made, xe tilted xir head at me and smiled. Did xe know?

It was just as extra as I thought it'd be.

Xe came to rest at that central seat. The guitar began playing on a loop of its own accord, light tinkling notes that reverberated. 'Welcome,' xe said in a far deeper voice than I was prepared to hear, 'to the faces I have seen and those I am yet to know. It takes courage to continue on a path of self-discovery; especially one that's difficult with no visible end goal. But you are here, and you have faith that between Mr Suresh and I, we might yet illumine that way for you as long as you ask yourselves: will you fall, or will you float?'

'Float,' they chorused back, me a step slower.

'Will you fall, or will you float?'

'Float,' bang in sync this time.

Xe walked, resting at each pair asking that same refrain 'fall or float'. And we floated every time.

'Fall or float?' it had come to be my turn and I met xir eyes.

'Float,' I said.

'And why do you want to float?' xe asked me; entirely unprepared for a second, *additional*, layer of questioning.

Because? Because falling sounds like the worse of the two options. Xe was being rhetorical, right? Everything seemed to slow down as all attention and eyes were on me. A glance in any direction met a face waiting for my answer. Ugh, why me?

'Why do you want to float?'

'Nobody else was asked this!' I contested.

'Nobody else is new,' xe said, 'or isn't here for themselves.' How could xe possibly know that? The pairs, the circle, had shrunk around us, pulled inward so we were surrounded. The musical drone had climbed in pitch; it left my ventricle, raw, and found a new home at the back of my throat. I'd been sensitive to sound for as long as I had memories; keenly at the mercy of anything with tempo and meaning beneath it. Receptive, my whole body was a vessel that matched the frequency exposed to it. I couldn't think for the sound, the tugging and the needling of my insides. The lump forming in my throat made me think of Selena and Tosin. Stand-ins for the people countless of the repatriated had lost to criteria we didn't have a sundamned clue about or had a say in.

'Because the alternative is to become nothing,' I choked out. Xe moved closer, and I took that as approval to continue, 'because falling is all a lot of us have done for the last few years. Because our old home fell and we were just supposed to take to this new home without a single problem. Because my sister fell when the Earth fell. Because I can't find one of my best friends and without him, I would've fallen years ago. Because life on the ground sucks, gravity is the great boner killer, and to float means I'm doing something about it. Because then I have a say in not sinking to the unknowable bottom of misery. Because I can put off that reunion if it is inevitable, or I can entirely avoid it if it is in my power.' In the time my tirade fell out of my mouth, xe held me in that same handshake as the suit. Those points of contact, the fingertip on my arm, our foreheads, I felt soothed, carried, seen, understood.

'My name is Esme and I will try to help you float, Elerie.' Only I could hear xir voice. Xe pulled back to regard the group, and I already missed the connection we'd formed. 'Now that we know why we float, I want us all to engage in solo work tonight. Find a space anywhere in the complex. When you have found somewhere you are happy with, activate your key once again, and it will guide you through the exercises.' My feet didn't want to move anywhere. They liked the spot I was in, how we felt just moments before. I sat where I stood, and Esme clutched xir hands and offered me a bow. The others filed out and when it was just me in the atrium, I realised the strings had left my insides. My throat empty, I coughed and I shouted vowel sounds just to reacquaint myself with my body.

I crossed my legs and held the gold cube key in my lap. It pulsed with my breathing, it expanded and contracted with my lungs.

'It's peaceful, isn't it?' It really is. I looked up and saw 'Mr Suresh' sat opposite me. He looked solid.

'You're not really here, are you?' I asked.

'No, no I'm not physically, but in here,' hand to his chest, 'and here,' the same hand to his head, 'I am there with you.'

'It's... been a long time, Jonah.' I matched his smile. It hurt that I was talking to another projection of him, but at least this one was closer to the real thing.

'Such a long time. You're so different now. I'm glad to have finally met you.'

I whipped my hair from side to side in thanks. 'And I think you're much the same; somehow I don't mean that disrespectfully. Also, Anderr!' I snapped my fingers at him. 'I used Renard to come here tonight.'

Jonah scratched the back of his head. 'An old habit. Gotta represent how this all started.'

'Are you any closer to the truth they don't want us to know?' I leant in, dropped my voice to a whisper.

'I'm always closer, I'm always further away. The search is continual and it's aspirational and it can never be completed. To know that is one of the most important steps for any truthseeker.'

'To know that you might never know everything?'

'No, nothing so grand and defeatist like that. That you can know and not know in complete harmony. We view knowledge as the quantifying, the rendering finite the impossible vastness of the world around us. Instead we know so we can return to where we came...' he trailed off.

'What?' I cocked my head at him.

'Old Ele would've interrupted me. Said I was full of shit!'

'What can I say? I've growed up.' I stuck my tongue

out at him. 'I came here to know what I don't, because I think that will make me fear less and understand more.'

Jonah nodded and nodded. 'We might never get the answer for why it was us that were uplifted to Aurin, and not others. We are allowed to resent and hate this fact of ourselves.'

'I still want to know though, Jo.'

'Of course you do, Elerie. If you know, will that cause you to fall or float?'

I looked down at the cube like it would give me an answer. When I was ready to respond, I looked up, but Jonah Suresh had already disappeared. I snickered.

When I'd sweated my way back home, I collapsed onto my bed feeling lighter for the evening's outcome. Esme invited us all back to the same place next week, and I told xir I'd be there. When I was just about ready to give into sleep, I received a ping. I tapped on my spex and it was another data transfer. It was young Jonah's entry on me from the Aurin Audit. It said that the new world wouldn't need me, and came with an apology from present-Jonah. Still salty after all this time. Jonah was as full of shit as he'd ever been, and I fell asleep warmer for it. In spite of what awaited me on the horizon. At least, now, I knew I deserved to float. No matter what.

[illegible]

[illegible] and more.

Jonah nodded and nodded. [illegible] never get the answer for why it was us that [illegible] and not others. We are allowed to [illegible] and [illegible] the [illegible].

I still want to know though, Jo.

Of course you do, Flora! If you know, [illegible] you [illegible]?

I looked down at the [illegible]. I would [illegible] to answer. [illegible] was ready to respond. I [illegible] up, but Jonah [illegible] had [illegible].

[illegible]

[illegible] and I [illegible] there [illegible] ready to [illegible] on the [illegible] it was [illegible] young [illegible] the [illegible] world [illegible] me, and [illegible] from [illegible] At [illegible]

[illegible]

PRE-FLIGHT, RED LIGHT. Buckets on laps. Gunny going through the motions again. I have half an ear to give him, though. I was mostly thinking about the wealth of data India gave me, and by extension the whole team. I lost a week. She didn't check in like I assumed she would. No adult supervision. I have pockets that I have to chain, impact zones that I'm gonna get the Jameses to take me through. We'd have to break rank and formation to do it. We Speeds are allowed to adapt in-play as long as we didn't leave a gaping hole a rival Speed couldn't also use. I'm wearing a new tail today too. I had to twist Joe's arm for it. He's our quartermaster and he wants to be very close with our cloudchaser. I, for one, happened to know that Polly our cloudchaser was looking to get close to someone who closely fit Joe's description. I said I'd see what I could do. What I didn't say was that it was Ava that matched the description. I watched it happen;

too many times. But he didn't need to know that, right? Hope's a great motivator, but sex is *much* better. So if you're hoping for sex, well... India ain't the only one capable of hatching schemes!

Every practice since I met India, I took the time to consult with the others on the team. Piece by piece, I shared her intel as nondescriptly as I could. It wasn't like I could publicise exactly what I had. Instead I took a behavioural therapist's approach. I asked, asked, asked, questions and allowed my audience to come up with the answers themselves. India didn't say I *couldn't* share something of what she gave me. And, besides, it's not like I could beat them on my own, right? Call it improvisation. Call it strategy. While watching film, spotting someone in the weight room, in the showers after practice, I spent time with people in the squads that I knew—and that I knew would listen to me—to spread the joy and the good news. Anyone I didn't think would listen to me, I hoped my allies could get through to them. If they had to keep my name out of their mouths, then that was fine.

They wouldn't know it was because of me now, but in-game, that was a whole different story.

Now I was sporting a faster tail and a new flight suit packing less weight with sterner glider flaps. I would be less able to take a hit, but Greys would be even less able to catch me in one of these. It just about passed regs. India's design was precise and bent where I was convinced it would break. I shouldn't have been surprised, what with where the schematics came from. I was trading durability for speed, a lighter polymer weave plus a slight fin in the middle of my back for aerodynamism. There wasn't a lot we could do to shield my brain from the gees, beyond not taking part at all, so it was dependent on me adapting to the lighter fabrication. It was another loan I had to take from the team, from Gunny, to make the changes to my suit. To add what I'd already owed in match fees and disciplinary action. Well, stick to the plan, Ele, and you'll more than pay what you owe him!

Hyperventilating returned today but for way different reasons this time. Progress is baby steps. My bucket lay on its side in my lap and, under three gees once more, I surveyed the crews as best as I could. New faces, some again with beards—ugh—and bruised faces from the last game.

The earbuds came out with the blue light. I did my neck-saving tactic and smiled when I saw more Tadpoles following suit. Once the bud was in, I prepared myself for Gunny's briefing and how much of it I was gonna ignore.

"Surprise, Ele!" That was *India*. Did I really think she wouldn't linger, chaperone me during her big plan? "Hide your surprise and act like it's Gunny's sweet, sweet gravel pouring into your ear with approach vectors, tactics and how you need to win so you all can eat and not feel like sacks of shit. Now if you're anything like I remember, you didn't sleep (I didn't much), you barely ate a thing (oh you bet I ate, Sun, just thinking about that cheese bowl), and you stink (that's not fair), but you've committed all that treasure to memory. Can you *believe* what I got you? I bet you can't; I just bet you can't! You can thank me later.

"The Royals have been dominating the league all season; you know it, I know it. But how you ask? Well, I'll tell you, my sweaty poppet. The Royals are being bankrolled from on-high. Higher-rollers you could say. Ones that built the Ombros, ones that put my net worth to shame. They keep warm and cool at the same time, all year round, and never need to descend from their existence atop the clouds." I'd heard her angry at Nox, but this sounded different. Elemental, like she felt down to her core. I knew the rich and fancy attacked each other, played at damaging lives like it was sport, but I thought that's just what they did, y'know? Like it wasn't that deep, they'd be laughing and tittering in Ombros soon enough, marvelling at whatever sharp cut the victor made over their victim.

But India was like me once. Like Selena, like Tosin. With the appropriate capacity for grudges, pettiness; she wouldn't, couldn't, mistake that mask of wealth as her actual face. Hearing her now proved that to me. That India had climbed to the top, but she wasn't one of them. "I don't have long before you start bottoming out; stick to the plan I mapped out for you and keep this comm channel open that I can hop on. Stay cool, stay loose, and don't wipe out, would you, Ele dear?" Her voice disappeared, and Gunny came in, but the close of his briefing made no sense out of context. The Greys had already shot into the warm sky assembling at the edge of the course, attitude jets along their flight suits priming them into ready positions. Teams 2 and 3 shot out and I could hear the Jameses chattering away on comms about what formations the Speeds needed to run today. They weren't including me in the chat, though. All the Speeds were nattering away. Nobody asked me.

But I couldn't tell them I was going to almost single-handedly bring down the most dominant team in the league.

And, if India was to be believed, topple a fucking *empire*...

Everything hurts.

Everything hurts and I don't think India's plan is going to plan. Not that the rest of the team know, or care for that matter. We're four splits into a game with the unbeatable Royals and we aren't getting completely eaten. To still be in play at this point was a miracle, but something in me hoped India's big plan was to give us such an edge that we'd crush them. But no. It's keeping us in step; making the game just about competitive enough. Playing some long, strategic, chess move, patience, who blinks first, duel-type shit is not my energy and it's setting my teeth on fucking edge! What makes this all worse is that the bearded guy from last week didn't die last game either. The one thing I ask for and I don't get it.

Most games are decided by how many splits you own, but occasionally, if you have super-fast times, but fewer splits by the end, sometimes you hold onto the win. As a Speed, we Surf the air from impact zone to impact zone where we get an explosion of additional speed—something about the constant sun altering wind pressure yadda yadda yadda—where you meet Slip teams like the Jameses who catch and throw us for that added kick. It's why our times are the quickest and the most valuable. Escorts take care of the boosting Slip teams the most—but have double duty for the rest of the squad—and Greys Surf slower than Speeds and their sole purpose is to get us: physical trauma given personality and intentionality. Why someone thought they were a *good* idea, I will never know. A Grey is why I can't move my left arm without aggravating what's most likely shattered nerve endings. I'm already trying to stay conscious under the constant gravity changing as it is.

We run formations to defend our Speeds and Slips between impact zone holds before the next split is live. It gets messy; sometimes, some poor shit doesn't turn off their comm when they collide with something, or meet a Grey, and you get to hear some ungodly wailing before Gunny in the plane—or anyone's Gunny equivalent—can take them off comms.

Off comms: that's what I wish India was right now. She must be following the game somehow because she keeps telling me what I'm doing wrong. How much faith she was putting in my skills. What's at stake. If we win. If she loses. Not us, *her*. I'm engaging my left and right brains in a big way as I have the Speed channel in one ear, relaying impact zone coordinates from Polly and trash talking the Royals for team morale. In the other ear, the naysaying, reprimanding India Palmer feeling the need to point out all of my problems as if I didn't already have intimate knowledge of them. I was clinging to the last active split, fiddling with my on-suit medkit, trying to get a shot of adrenaline into my paralysed left arm. I could hear my sister as an unwelcome third voice, all mother-mode in my head. Telling me the dangers, how I'd end up a drooling wreck. It's weird because it *is* outlawed—everyone knows it—but at the same time we still get games off every week. Sure, there's the logistics of finding airspace that doesn't clash with flight plans, be it transport, drone deliveries, or the military. The cloak and dagger of firing decoy buoys at different locations so the authorities are scrambled to dummy areas giving us a neat window to play and finish a game. Yet we *still* play.

Maybe India's right. Maybe there is more to this than we know.

The shot goes in without a hitch. My teeth are clenched as I jab the painkiller in as well. There's a warm sensation that tingles my body over, and I feel a surge of energy. The urge to just push off indiscriminately is strong, but I hold on as the next split is active in a couple of minutes and my backup's got their hands full. I had podium level times through each split so far, and this split I was second. Gunny is all profanity and pragmatism. He's been in the game a while, a bona fide old-timer, but he forgets to go off-comm when he utters that he's never seen anything like this. The Royals are a ballet company, synchronised swimmers, a hive mind, all rolled into one. Their Speeds are almost undetectable to the eye and the HUD of my goggles also struggle to see them. Their Greys are HUGE, like leviathan huge, and I swear to the sun they move just as fast as I do. I used to think that the Jameses were the peak of understanding, but they've got Slips who seem to know where the impact...

Fuck.

I'm straight on the comms. "Jameses. I think their Slips know where the impact zones are ahead of time."

"You've gotta be..."

"...shitting me."

"I've got an idea, but it's really, really fucking *stupid*," I say and I'm already thinking about how in the million ways under the sun it could go wrong.

"Let's hear it!"

"Yes, Ele, really, I'm all ears." Eeuuuggghhhhhhh India. I feel like she's a creepy uncle right now, lingering and not getting the obvious hint to back off.

"I think they're doing more than predicting the impact zones. Either their cloudchaser has some intimate sunblessed knowledge we don't know about, or they're *making* impact zones." The silence told me I had their undivided attention, and I continued with my stupid plan. "When the next split comes active, I'm gonna come straight for you Jameses, but I don't want you to launch me towards the split. I want you to shoot me straight at their largest assembled Slip team. I'll turn my transponder off too, fly blind, and hopefully they'll treat me like their own."

"Ride in their slipstream?"

"Like a parasite in their asshole, I love it!" James the Better had the worst associations, I swear.

"Ele, I might be a layman, but I know a doomed plan when I hear one. Flying without a transponder sounds like suicide. Have you got a death wish?"

"It's suicide for most, India, and if mine's on, they'll know I'm a Tadpole and some Grey will eat me."

"They won't be able to detect you?"

"*No one will.*" I switched back to the Speed channel. "Bellamy and Darius, I'll need a Delta scrub heading straight for the next split the moment it's active. Our reserve Slips are at point two and they'll run it fast."

"*You* want a scrub? The hell are you thinking, Elerie?" That's Gunny. "I make you a starter and now you wanna tell me how to do my job, is that it you little shit?"

"Don't be like that, Gunny, *trust* me! If it doesn't work, you only lose me..."

"Don't forget your scrub. Or d'you think you're worth more than them?"

Fuck. I was really glad Gunny was a pro and was talking to me like this on a direct channel rather than over the teamwide comm. I *hate* being made a public fool of.

"We still have the reserve Escorts; draft some of them in, give them that military spiel you know so well. Giving themselves up for the man and woman fighting beside them."

"...Elerie..." his response was a little delayed so I think I was wearing him down. As long as his ego withstood the suggestion.

"We can't beat them if we're just playing by our playbook. I'm going full Icarus on this next play." So when I was talking about the silence before, it had shit on this next one. I could only hear the wind and my ragged breathing for a good twenty seconds.

SPLIT LIVE IN 15. The alert took me back to the night at Virtual Freeality and when my feed got hijacked. I know data protection meant the owners couldn't see what their clients got up to. Yo, we would've been had if they do snoop. I mean, everyone *knows* Ultsurf, and it really wouldn't surprise me if other people played the game in their fantasy. But we had actual players forming the architecture of our session. So if they did look, and saw how accurate ours was...

One worry at a time, though. I was seconds away from this plan really kicking into gear, and if I was going to have any second thoughts, I didn't have long to entertain them.

"You heard her, get Elerie the scrub she wants, Escorts give her a ten-metre chevron the moment you think you see her!" Gunny, you beautiful man!

SPLIT LIVE IN 10. We're tied at two splits apiece and the only way we'd get a lead to protect is if this pays off.

What am I thinking?

SPLIT LIVE IN 5. Could I really do it? Could I beat the Royals? Cheat the cheats?

Could we win?

"And make it look good, boys!" Me.

SPLIT ACTIVE. The frenzy ensues the moment every transponder is pinged the next split. The blue lights of the gate when you fix on it, dependent on how good your cloudchaser is, determines a flight plan that's continually corrected with every act you do. It's really useful and saves lives. But the moment I hit the Jameses' zone,

I'm flying without it. All the teams are crying out their formations, course correcting with the cloudchaser's data. I kick off the gate and glide towards the impact zone where I'm sure I'll meet my men. Bellamy and Darius are arrowing from point two in my scrub and I hope to the sun they stay cool and don't wipe out. I've never really spent a lot of time with Bellamy outside, but it was sweet that she took me home that night, made that sunblessed breakfast for the ages. Maybe I'd get her to do it again, just without secret meetings and me drooling like an infant as an entrée. And when she rested her head on my shoulder for those few seconds before we ate... made me warm in all the right places. Darius said something funny which we all laughed at, and I doubly hoped they stayed cool.

There it is. The impact zone. Like floating fire. Darius explained it to me once. The sun altering wind pressure creates little pockets where the temperature in the air is ripe, made ready to explode. Like a geyser in the air, he said. Via a process significantly more error than trial, the nerds behind Ultsurf's tech created the Speed's flight suits to siphon that energy and repurpose it into thrust as we pass through. The Jameses are spinning around it, antagonising it. For Slippers, their suits emit a low energy pulse from a jet on their back, designed to prolong the impact zone's time to release. The pulse makes them shimmer ever so slightly and also makes them a pain to get a hold on. I wanna say that's where they got their name from, but please don't quote me on that.

I set myself into a ball and slowly rotate. I have a few moments, a calm before the storm where I can think, okay Ele you've had your fun, maybe back out, maybe treasure your life, maybe don't do this. Once their hands were on me, feet planted on my back, all the clever, self-preserving thoughts had to get the fuck out.

"You're really stupid, Elerie."

"Absolutely sunkissed like laundry left out too long!" parting gifts, the last things I hear over the comms as I deactivate my transponder. For a little while my eyes are closed, and when I open them, it is *just the sky*. No flight plans, windspeed, radar, nothing. The sky, clouds, that ever-present sun, and the dots of people moving far and close by. My eyes are watering, but I can't tell if I am overwhelmed by the freedom or scared out of my mind at my impending death. I have to judge the distance between me and the Royal Slips, and risk a look to my right to see my Escort chevron. Blessed, they can see me. Behind them our Greys fly right at them, batons out, hungry for blood. They had to look like they were after me, a rogue element, a Royal spun far out of formation due to a faulty suit, so when I rendezvous—

The lurch of being caught by hands.

I point at my helmet and draw my hand across my neck. The Slips look at each other, back at me, and sign something that looked like "can you believe this rookie?" and "why us?" Great, they believe me. Another thing in India's care package was the Royals' signing dictionary. Memory games are never my strong suit and I'm wracking my brain for things I need to say that I have to make sure aren't Tadpole.

Veered off course. No transponder. Want at split. I point at the active split to hammer it home.

Not your turn, rook. Krjnwoenf Unit are first. Then rgeigrwg. Garbled; look I didn't remember all their stupid unit names, okay? I'm not proud.

Need split time. Bonus for food. Broke. Please.

Against formation. The Tadpoles are decent for a pack of inbred fucks.

By the sun, please?

Ejprignrgnwfdf.

What?

Ejprignrgnwfdf. Deal or not?

Ugh, there it is. Probably asking me to join a historical re-enactment group specialising in eighteenth century ballroom dancing. To pay their rent. That they could haze me to sort out all the repairs and cleaning of the suits. Oh, who gives a shit! It wasn't like I was a Royal. Or that I would redeem whatever I'd just agreed to. *Sure. What you want, you have.* They high-five and signalled to the other Slips. I'd have given myself a self-five if I wanted to risk the mobility of my arm. They agitate the impact zone whilst one of them drifts directly into the middle of it, and I see my death. This is how I die. No joke. Whoever they are, their flight suit looks modified, bulkier than it should be, and I see why. They have a jet on their back that's firing sporadically into the eye of the impact zone. Another Slip drifts over and holds something in their hands that I swear to the sun looks like one of those pneumatic drills.

I was right. They are *making* their own sundamned impact zones.

So your cloudchaser has a heat map of the game area. If you get a numbers human in that position, they work off stats and probabilities; reactive, basically. Calling coordinates for impact zones with barely any margin for explosion. Sometimes they'd even misfire, and if you've sent your Slips over for a dud, they yell at you, your Gunny yells at you, and your opponent gets a head start on you to redeploy on another. But our Polly was on her way to a doctorate in meteorology. She liked to ping zones that with a little Slip agitation could be primed for that Speed conversion. A slightly longer game, yes, but you rarely fought an opposing Slip team for a zone they deemed to be yellow over a red zone. But if you could turn a cold zone to an impact zone, you could control the game area no problem. No opposing player would waste their time fighting over cold unless they really had their bloodlust up, and so the Royal Slips could work unimpeded. I wish I could've activated my HUD, watched the temperature readings, any kind of analytics that could explain exactly how the sundamned Royals were cheating.

Instead I have to shield my eyes and my face from whatever the fuck that drill is. The wind is loud in my ears, whistling, before inverting somehow. Like the sound of water going down a drain when you were only paying attention to the tap at the start. The edges of my vision seem to darken slightly, as energy is being pulled from all around us and channelled into the cold zone. This is how they maintain field and speed advantage over other teams. How they smuggled this huge fucking tech onto their planes, into the game area without any detection— this is what India was getting at. But I'm masquerading as a Royal, one of them. I have to look on at this shit like I knew it already. Yesterday's news. Unremarkable. Boring because can we win already?

Okay, okay. Imagine looking at a bird's eye view of a tornado, that raging, roiling, natural force. Now think about idiot humans making that thing worse. That's what I'm looking at. It scares the shit out of me, but I have to launch off it like I love it. The Slips continue agitating the zone, all with those jets on their backs and getting a smooth orbit of it. Two other Slips form their launchpad similar to the Jameses, and I tuck into my ball.

This.

Feels.

Like.

My.

Skin.

Is.

Peeling.

Off.

And I'm ashamed to say I fucking love it!

I'M OUT OF the ball and don't think I have long before I have to turn my transponder on. I wish I could see the faces of the Royal Slips when they realise how I played them. To the Sun, I wish it. My target, the active split, is an ascent away, but without access to my data, getting there in one piece is scarily down to my own skill... Ignoring advice and common sense for the sake of glory.

If anyone wants to ask me, I'd say the Icarus title was a little too on the nose.

The Surf

Another bonus of hurtling towards my certain death with no transponder means I don't have to listen to India. I don't know how many games she's watched, so I don't know how useful her input really is. I course correct, moved my arms into a crooked position a lot like tucked wings, and give my attitude jets a little squirt, hoping I'll either get to the split sooner than the poor scrub, or not that far behind the Royal Speeds. I've gotta line of sight my corrections and I feel another sunkissed batch of doubt and worry and rapidly approaching mortality. I risk a look at the chevron again. They're fully engaged with the Royals now, dots of varying sizes colliding and rolling around with each other. That's their job and it was Gunny's call, so I don't feel completely bad about their fate. The Delta scrub, though. I'm not gonna be able to recognise them without my transponder active, but the eye test would be looking out for the bodies, basically. A scrub's a decoy. A dummy formation of crewmembers designed to trick the opposing to deploy a proportionate force to halt whatever it is they were trying to do. Our Delta scrub was a squad of six Slips and two Speeds. A configuration that would tell the Royals we were primed to make a dash for the live split. If we could get enough of their Greys chasing ghosts, I might just make it through this split and back into our controlled game area before they had a chance to mobilise against me. Because they would; I can't score without my transponder on. And once I turn that back on, the Royals will know exactly who I am.

Once I shoot past a point I'm guessing is a half-klick from the split, I reactivate my transponder and took a moment to process all the pollution of my HUD. And the noise, by the Sun, the noise!

When a transponder is rebooted, all the comm channels are made active. Diagnostic contingency, we're told. It's all agony, strategy, and profanity. Gunny is yelling coordinates and plays, and the Jameses are trying to keep the Slip teams alive, rotating defence on impact zones, leaving enough players to kick anyone who needs to bug out. And enough to control holding the zones from the Royals. James the Lesser is also yelling that the Royals are fucking cheating. Any ounce of Phalanx-doubt gone when we heard his passion. Cloudchaser Polly is trying to keep the steady flow of zones communicated, and the Escorts are moaning sunawful noises of pain. It takes me some time to get the onboard system to drown out all that was unnecessary. The flight plan kicks in and I can see I misjudged the distance... by some distance. I have seconds to alter my trajectory to hit the split. I have even fewer seconds to notice that the chevron, and—oh Sun—the scrub too, the Royals have binned going for them and they're now after me!

And of course, so is India. Like an itch I can't reach.

"Ele, where have you *been*? Have I been talking to myself all this time?" I don't have time to reply. I'm through the split and my time is pinged in the top right of my sight. The score is *big*. I'm the fastest Speed through now. It pings Tadpole teal and we own it. I own it. I wish I could see the look on the faces of those Royal Slips when they realise they catapulted us, me, into the lead. Whatever I gave up for the pleasure would be nothing on whatever forfeit they would experience.

The Surf

Not a single part of me felt anything like sympathy. Gunny is whooping, congratulating me and surprised I'm still alive. He urgently tells the scrub to bug out, worried he's too late. I fire my jets on full blast in front of me so I can slow down and think what to do next. I'm deep in enemy territory, and without a Slip team to give me a good kick outta here, it'll be like front crawling away from rocket-powered jet skis. I don't like my odds. I never liked swimming. It's not that I *can't* swim. There are just so many other things I'd rather do with my time.

When we left Earth, Mother and me, one of the relocation criteria was whether the child demonstrated any physical or intellectual proficiency worth sponsoring on the new world. For the three-year waiting list, she threw everything at me. I played every conceivable sport with tutelage in days without practice in order to unearth whatever intellectual curiosities were embedded in my head. I felt privileged and tested on for the duration. All that was missing was some kind of microscopic evaluation. I'm surprised she didn't test me for fertility. She believed there was something inherent inside me and whilst my performance at most things was evidence towards a sunkissed disappointment, she persevered. Maybe that's why we fell out of contact. Aurin was our new home eventually, but through no sponsored thanks on my part. We waited the three years. My mother had to hustle to get a good job. Our life worked. She got a position in infrastructure; promoted from a lowly administrator in an office to city planning for the nascent communities that were opening monthly. It wasn't exciting to my young brain which, now I think about it, was *insane*. Sunkissed in every definition. She had a team. I mean, it wasn't like she built cities on her own. I used to think it was all just 'we should put a park over here,' but she went so deep, she had 3D printed models of sewage systems, mass transit schedules were the only wallpaper in her bedroom, and I swear to the sun there are pictures of me in front of toys with less happiness than she had with her work.

I sighed. At the dissolution of our relationship. I could've tried harder. Really, I could've. But she also could've met me halfway. Should've. The whole family didn't get to move. When the relocation clearance arrived, Selena wasn't on the list. They were splitting us up. I cried for days. Selena, bless her, didn't fight and spit and curse and scream like I wanted to. She helped me pack, helped me revise for the tests. Told me I could live my life the way I felt inside there. That it'd be easier. She taught me about adjusting my body clock to keep to the 24-hour Earth cycle because Aurin was sunlight all the time. She said I was young enough to adapt to it easier than she ever could. She had to be lying; there was nothing I could do easier than her. Continued mothering me when my actual mother went AWOL. I didn't, couldn't, understand then. I was a child. The world wasn't fair and now the new world we were moving to seemed just as mean. What was the point of starting somewhere new if it was gonna be just as shit? No, worse. Without Selena, what was the point in *anything*?

Didn't they test Selena and realise that she was infinitely better at everything than me? Not coming to

Aurin amounted to a death sentence deferred. They told us that the Earth was dying. Selena said she was going to stay and figure out how to save it, so I could come and visit her in the future. When I asked Selena if she could visit us, our mother said she couldn't and told me to stop asking so many childish sundamned questions. I'd never heard her swear before. Not once.

I think she blamed me from that point on. Little things at first. We memorialised Selena in different ways. I held photos, keepsakes, tangible memories; my mother talked about Selena to her staff, her new friends. And I always heard the unspoken barbs. Her perfect daughter was left on a dying world, and she'd come to Aurin with me, who had to pass a test to just be her daughter in the first place. We lost contact with Selena before everyone lost contact with Earth. That's when the little things grew. As soon as I knew it was possible, I moved out. There was no blowout, no huge flashpoint or confrontation. I just took myself out of my mother's life and moved her out of mine. It was that simple. She was still alive; that much I knew. Retired to an algae farm in the arms of some gene wizard who helped make the planet's food. Seven years we haven't spoken and she wasn't only controlling my diet, but those of planets. Nothing like a glow up on multiple global scales. Maybe I should've called her last week when I thought about it. And if I wiped out today, she'd either never know or discover her daughter was a criminal the same time she was dead. Confirmation that I would never be Selena. No matter how hard I'd tried to change. No, to the Sun with that. So *morbid*. So miserable. I'd made something of myself and I wasn't dead yet! I could still make it back to our team, through the shit, and come out the other side not a vegetable.

And then it hits me.

Tosin.

They didn't let him come to Aurin either. India had a Selena-hurt of her own.

"Okay India, you're great, and I *love* that we can chat like this, but I'm gonna need you to shut the fuck up." I smile to myself when I add, "no disrespect." Here I am executing her plan and I'm scared to tell her that I know. That I understand. That she hurt like I hurt and she's not alone. That we are the same. High-roller status aside. Would that even matter to her if I said it? Maybe win first, pull off this victory, then maybe see about having a heart-to-heart with India fucking Palmer.

Hop onto the team comm. It's a mixture of shock and awe at the massive spike in our points and the drop from the Royals, and cursing from the injuries we'd sustained. The reserve Escorts are being scrambled in and the Delta scrub, ugh, less time thinking about them, the better. There's one split left in the game. We dodn't need to score higher to win after my Icarus paid off. I wish I could see the data miner's face right about now. When they were giving me shit.

'Oh I'm not so impressed with what I see, Elerie.'

'Oh I don't think you can pull this off, Elerie.'

'Oh I have no fun and I probably have as much social grace as a trash incinerator, Elerie.'

Well, My Great Doubting Data Miner. Here I am, pulling off India's top-secret coup with all my problems, beating the sundamned Royals. So who's laughing now?!

But if the Royals were anything like me, scraping me off their batons was more important than the victory now. Maybe I should be doing less laughing, more planning how to make it out alive.

I once heard a rumour of a player who could mask their transponder signal. Not just turn it off, but they could *clone* it too. Make it look like they were on another team at any given moment. If I was that player, I could bounce my signal all over the field so the Royals couldn't keep an eye on me. But I also learned not to believe everything you hear when, at ten, I got told by Mackenzie Lewis that everyone on Aurin was yellow because of the permanent suntanning. When I got to Aurin, I was embarrassingly shocked to find out she was making shit up. But maybe there was something to use in them being able to track me...

"Polly, could you show me the quickest way I could get back to our guys?" I ask into silence. Instead, a flight path shows up, indicating which impact zones I could ride off on my own. It takes me dangerously close to Royal territory. Just my unlucky luck.

"Maybe a route where I won't get totally eaten?" The flight path winks out and comes back without an even degree changed. I get the point. My HUD tells me we are deep into our reserves and almost everyone is engaged in something to the tune of a) not dying or b) not getting their asses kicked. Add to that the next split is bound to be active soon. I look at my fuel stock. Low. But least my arms aren't as completely useless as before. Apparently, once upon a time, flight suits didn't have field medkits on them, and I shudder at the thought of having a popped-out elbow forty thousand feet in the air and forty thousand feet away from any sort of medical attention. I need another wise idea. Not Icarus-level wise but something to get back in play.

I get it. "Gunny, can you waypoint me to the nearest Royal Slip team?"

"More sunkissed insanity from my no-good Speed?" he chucks my way.

"No-good except helping take down the *Royals*."

"I want answers about that too."

"Another time, waypoint please?" It takes a few seconds, and eyes full of static, but the suit computer outlines possible flight paths like it was supposed to. I need one of their agitators. If I can get it back to our plane, I'll have proof of the Royals being shit and it'd give me the boost I'd need to achieve that. I have no choice. Firing my jets, I tuck my arms in to missile at the nearest Slip team. I watch the dots hover and rotate around the impact zone they're creating. My suit gives me all it had; warning signs flash up about fuel levels and the gees I'm pulling, but I have to close the distance between me and the Slips as soon as possible… before they hurtle flying death at me. I reactivate the flight path back to our guys once I'm convinced I can line of sight towards the Slips. I'm not really sure how I'll get an agitator off of one of their Slip teams, but I don't get a sundamned second to think about it. Once my suit pings, the Greys lock onto my position. A lot of them. Oh, they know who I am now, and there's no way they'll let me make it through the game alive. Sun, let them come! They won't scare me now, not now that I've all but beaten them. I'll run head first into their attack and I'll piss defiance in the wind. Gambling on their singular purpose as their undoing, I head for the edge of their advancing formation. As expected, they adjust their flight plans to form a claw coming right for me, and to make sure any point of avoiding contact was impossible.

Which suits me just fine. I have no plans to run.

India's care package showed me how their Greys liked to control the space they clashed in with rival teams. A lot of it came with synchronising their suits all hive mind. And their claw formation worked like a bullet: once fired, it couldn't be unfired. Crucially, it also couldn't *turn* like I can solo. Correcting on my trajectory meant they've showed their hand and have to see it out. Maybe they thought I'll get scared at being outnumbered—and I am—but I'm also in control. With my left arm outstretched, I squirt a blast from the jet to get a quick spiralling rotation: starting my own bullet that can't be unfired.

COLLISION IN 10.

SPLIT ACTIVE IN 20.

My mother's face flashed before my eyes. Tosin. Selena. My first roommate. My first kiss.

COLLISION IN 5.

What the Greys don't know is that *my* bullet can turn.

I see them all, hands out, batons out, ready to eat me alive, and my suit gives me that little bit of juice saved in reserve for a manoeuvre like this. When you picture a claw, there are gaps between the fingers, or talons, or whatever the thing is. Slim, but they're there. The Royals' claw have one such gap that I'm aiming for. My spiral means reading my flight plan would be hard for them, and with their bloodlust up, they'll only have eyes on the prize I've apparently served. The Grey on the edge—think the tip of a thumb pointed right at you—their kit looks heavier than the rest. At the last moment, I stop my spiral as I slip past them, and kick off their passing body.

SPLIT ACTIVE.

I'm going in completely the wrong direction to the next active split, but I am headed right for an undefended Slip team. With their agitators. And their floating fires. With those fucking high-rolling Royal fucks eating my slipstream.

SOMETHING ELSE CATCHES my tired eyes, though. Beyond the immediate field of play, there are aircraft heading this way. I'm pretty sure us and the Royals were the only teams in play. In fact, the Royals *never* take a game against more than one team at any one point. During the entire sundamned season… another tally in the great conspiracy India told me about. They'd been late additions to games, stealing the last few splits, carving a huge swathe through times and taking all the glory. Something that seemed to happen indiscriminately without any hope of stopping. But what is this?

"Um, Gunny?"

"By the sun Elerie, how are you still alive? Why aren't you headed for the next—" his shock sounds like the relative of admiration.

"Less questions; more help please, Pawel. I'm sending you some coordinates." Tap, tap, tap, good thing the suit

The Surf

flight computer doesn't run on the same fuel. "Who else could be out here?" The whistle of air. The vague idea that India is waiting on the other comm losing her shit. The main team comm with Sun-knows-what mayhem currently unfolding. It feels like the storm before the storm. I haven't been calm for days. Not since North Ombro. Before India came back into my life *wanting* things from me. He isn't quiet for long.

"No idea, to be honest. What did you just call me— Sun, has our game been discovered?" His voice goes muffled. Probably barking orders to someone on the team bridge. Decoy buoys and bullshit chatter any two-bit data miner could find were our lines of defence for the sport we die playing. Did one of those fail? Did someone burn us? I fly past the Slip team responsible for the claw. Fleeting seconds where I have to glance and come up with an idea to steal an agitator from the other Slip team I'm heading for. "I'm opening a channel to them, one sec." Gunny cuts us off. The aircraft are still coming. Big fucking things. Big enough to hold other teams in there. Or Aurin's taskforces created to stop us. Or something else.

Before I have the chance to find out what Gunny said to them, there's a blinding flash and the worst concussion. My communicators scream decibels in my ears, and I get a neck full of whiplash as I pull gees close to knocking me right out. I can hear my suit squeal. Maybe groan. Crack? My HUD goes haywire and I can't focus on anything beyond a few feet. My eyes feel useless. Seared onto my eyelids is the afterimage of the gates being torn apart. Is everyone else dropping out of the sky like me? Wait, I can feel my altitude falling. I am dropping. I hold my arms out either side of me and I will more than activate the jets on my suit to get level. I feel like the altimeter in all plane disaster movies, the dial spinning like a fairground ride, the numbers falling so fast you could only really think in time to death rather than distance.

It takes me awhile to realise I can't hear myself speak. I'm yelling to Gunny about my situation, requesting a buoy, a bailout. Something. But I can't hear me; could he? My vision clears slowly; I can see as well as feel my limbs. None of them phantom, thank the Sun. I'm almost sick a couple of times. In my falling, though, I see a sight that makes me throw up for real. Debris. Human and plane. A slowly dispersing cloud of colour and wreckage that was once the Tadpole control plane. Gunny. There is another flash, and I watch two more gates explode. There are players in its vicinity, and they spin away from the impact like a doll suffering the wrath of a child. The new aircraft keep coming, and it's clear to me they are the cause of the carnage, of the death befalling my team. I try to switch to an emergency channel, to signal our people on the ground about what was happening, but I get no response. I try India? Nothing. That link had been severed too.

Ugh.

In every suit, for every team, there's a hardline connection to only use in case of an emergency. This sundamned qualified. It was a direct line to Aurin's law enforcement. It survived whatever damage my suit suffered and the destruction of our plane. I make a connection.

The Surf

"Thank the Sun, we need help. Gods, we need help—"

I hear the connection die.

No.

It got killed.

They are ignoring me. Turning me away.

Nobody is coming. Nobody cares.

As Tadpoles die around me and I hurtle to my death, I hope there is a grander reason for it.

ACKNOWLEDGEMENTS

IMAGINE ME SAYING this with Halle Berry Oscar acceptance crying energy:

Ed Wilson, my agent, for chasing me for two years convinced that I was a good writer. Everything cool happens on these pages because of you. A sartorially sharp bulwark against any doubts I've had.

Beth Lewis, for the lunches and gaming sessions where we chatted life and books. And for giving me the prompts that turned into this story. I can only remember two of them, but I swear I asked for three...

Zack Graham, for being my day one. The transatlantic calls and the time you devoted to helping me get this to where it is. Dead ass, he is my guy.

K. Angel, you have them to thank for the Virtual Freeality scene.

Anna Hickman and Tamsin Wressell, for a lot of the character work that's gone into Ele and the gang.

The slew of beta readers I foisted this upon, too numerate to count, but know that I appreciate you. Even the ones I don't speak to anymore.

To Mike Rowley, for seeing something in The Surf. A guiding touch that's made me a better writer. To Dave, and all of the Solaris team for giving a shit about novellas. Sunkissed, the lot of you.

To Tash Payne, you had my back so I could do this. Hold up.

FIND US ONLINE!

www.rebellionpublishing.com

/rebellionpub /rebellionpublishing /rebellionpublishing

SIGN UP TO OUR NEWSLETTER!

rebellionpublishing.com/newsletter

YOUR REVIEWS MATTER!

Enjoy this book? Got something to say?

Leave a review on Amazon, GoodReads or with your favourite bookseller and let the world know!